The Windvale Sprites

Mackenzie Crook is a hugely diverse actor who has played a wide variety of roles, from Ragetti in the first three record-smashing, swashbuckling *Pirates of the Caribbean* films, to the wonderful character of Gareth in *The Office* and the critically acclaimed Konstantin in the Royal Court's version of *The Seagull*.

The Windvale Sprites is his first book.

The Windvale Sprites

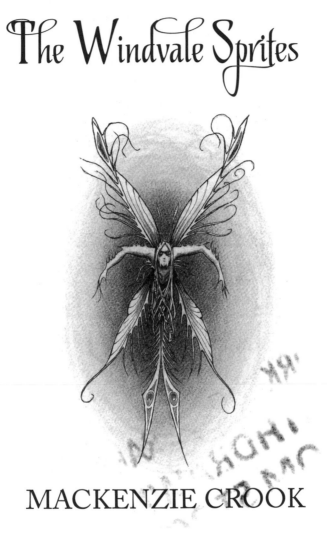

MACKENZIE CROOK

ff

faber and faber

7779928

First published in the UK in 2011
by Faber and Faber Ltd
Bloomsbury House
74–77 Great Russell Street
London WC1B 3DA

Printed in England by TJ International Ltd, Padstow, Cornwall

The right of Mackenzie Crook to be identified as the author and
illustrator of this work has been asserted in accordance with Section 77
of the copyright, Designs & Patents Act of 1988

A CIP record for this book
is available from the British Library

ISBN 978–0–571–24071–5

Prologue

When I was a boy there was a man by the name of Fish whose job it was to tell us his weather predictions.

Mr Fish was good at his job and though he never claimed to be 100 per cent accurate, we trusted his forecasts and adjusted our clothing accordingly.

That was until one day when a woman phoned Mr Fish in his place of work and told him that she suspected a hurricane to be on its way.

Now Fish took this badly. None of his machines had spotted a hurricane and he had some of the best and most expensive machines in the country. He *had* to, people trusted him.

So he went on television and not only told us what the woman had predicted but dismissed it with a scoff.

Reassured and amused we all went cosily to bed.

Only to be awoken by a monster.

To this day Mr Fish claims the storm that ripped across the country that night was not technically a hurricane but I reckon it was. The next morning the whole county was devastated. Roofs were gone from houses, leaving just the walls (and in some cases the four walls had been blown clean away leaving only the roof). Most of the trees in the area had been laid on their sides and the residents of Sevenoaks awoke to find only one of their famous oak trees still standing. Windows were smashed and those people who foolishly left their washing on the line overnight never saw their pants again.

I'm telling you this because it is on the night of that great storm that this story begins. For a week afterwards we had no electricity and so all the schools were shut. Mums and dads still had to go to work so we were left to ourselves during the days to go and explore this strange new landscape. What an exciting week that was, but none more so than for a boy called Asa Brown who, that first morning, made a discovery that would lead him on an extraordinary adventure.

1

The Storm

When Asa Brown thought back to the actual night of the storm he found he couldn't really remember it very well. He'd had a busy day previously and had fallen into bed exhausted. There he slept fitfully through noisy dreams of howling beasts and old steam trains until, eventually, he was woken by the sharp rap of a stick hitting his window. He vaguely remembered peering through the curtains but not being able to see anything clearly. It was so dark, unusually dark, there were no streetlights, no cars on the road and the rain was coming straight at the

windowpane. He lay back down and listened, for a while, to the tempest.

The raging wind was playing the houses and trees like the instruments of an orchestra, producing extraordinary noises. It whined and whistled, changed direction and dropped an octave, turned to the window and rattled the glass. Then it dropped silent for a second and crept back across the road to start again. Each time the wind slammed into the house it seemed to get louder until it reached a crescendo, when a terrifying bass note would kick in and make the house vibrate to its very foundations. Beneath this noise, Asa could make out the smashtinkle of greenhouse glass and toppling terracotta pots, with fence panels and gates banging out an idiotic rhythm.

Strange though it might sound, these noises eventually lulled him back into a deep sleep. The house was old and prone to making unearthly noises, which he was used to and the drone of the wind was not unlike being on a train. So he went back to dreaming of locomotives thundering through tunnels and slept that way until morning.

The next morning was calm by comparison. The hurricane was now a mere gale and was carrying out its final checks, seeing that everything was dislodged that could be dislodged, uprooted or simply repositioned.

Many power lines across the area had been blown down and so, as there was no electricity, school was closed. Asa lost no time in exploring the damage outside.

There was a large pampas grass deposited in the middle of the lawn like a giant, stranded jellyfish. It had probably been blown there from Mr and Mrs Singer's front garden at number 72. A television aerial was trying unsuccessfully to get a signal at the top of the Hawthorn.

Then he saw it. Floating amongst the duckweed at the edge of the fishpond was a small figure. Asa assumed that it was a toy that had been blown from somewhere else, why wouldn't he? But as his fingers closed around it he jumped back in horror for what he touched was not plastic or wood. It was skin.

He sat down with a bump on the wet grass with his back to the fishpond and tried to calm down. His heart was pounding and he felt shaky. Thank goodness there was nobody around to see him, he thought, he must have looked pretty silly. Slowly he turned back to the pond and looked over the tall iris leaves.

There it was, floating face up just a few feet away.

It had big eyes. Huge black eyes that were all pupil. It was skinny like a stick with extraordinarily long legs that were bent back unnaturally. Its slender arms ended in delicate hands and fingers that tapered to fine points.

It was hard to tell exactly how tall it was but it couldn't have been more than six inches long.

Asa crawled closer.

The creature had olive-brown skin with a seam of sharp-looking thorns running up the outside of each limb. It had dark wispy hair on its head from which sprouted two long antennae and pointed ears.

As Asa looked more closely he could see that the surface of its eyes were made up of countless facets that glittered in the light. The tiny face had a sharp chin and framed a small nose and an even smaller mouth. On the creature's chest was tattooed a design like a Celtic knot and its skin was covered in bruises and scrapes.

With heart thumping, Asa dipped his fingers into the water and underneath the creature. It was all he could do to stop freaking out as he lifted it out of the pond and deposited it on the bank, quick as he could.

It flopped on to its front on the grass and Asa saw, with amazement, that sprouting from its shoulder blades were four, slender, transparent wings. An intricate network of veins divided each

like a stained-glass window.

That is when the thought struck him. *I've found a fairy*. Just like that with no exclamation mark.

It's dead, but I am almost certain that I have found a real-life dead fairy. It suddenly all made sense. This is what 'fairies' are. Not wand-waving Tinkerbells but sinewy insect-men: wild creatures that must be very secretive and hardly ever spotted. This one must have been blown in the hurricane from the remote place where he lived and ended up in my fishpond.

Asa ran inside and found a shoebox to put the creature in; he didn't know quite what he was going to do with it but he knew he had to do *something*. He also had the presence of mind to grab his dad's old camera and, returning outside, he took snaps of the creature until the film was used up. It wasn't a great camera and the light was not good but at least you would be able to make something out.

Eventually he lifted the limp body into the box and took it back inside the house where he almost collided with his mum at the foot of the stairs.

'I just saw Chris's dad up the road and he said your school will be closed until the end of next week while they repair broken windows and roof tiles,' said Mum. 'Dad and I will be back at work on Monday so you'll have to occupy yourself until the end of the week. Don't forget to find out if your school trip is still going ahead next Sunday as we've bought all the stuff for it so I'll be annoyed if it's cancelled.'

The impending biology field trip had been hanging over Asa like a dark cloud for a couple of months. The entire class were off to some bleak cove for a week in a remote part of the country to study species of lichen growing on drystone walls. The stories told of this field trip in previous years were of seven days of crushing boredom. It was an endurance test just to make it through without going insane. Many boys, much tougher than Asa, ended up feigning illness and being picked up by their mums on day two.

But for now this was the last thing on his mind.

'OK,' said Asa and tried to slip past.

'Were you listening?'

'Yes,' Asa lied.

'If it is cancelled you'll just have to come with us to Grandma and Grandpa's.'

'OK.'

'What's in the box?'

Asa froze.

'What do you mean?'

Mum looked at him then the box.

'What's in the box?' she repeated.

'Oh! The shoebox!' Asa acted as though he'd forgotten he was holding it. 'Oh nothing, it's empty, I need it . . . for the school trip.'

Mum looked unconvinced but decided not to pursue it any further. Asa saw an opportunity and legged it up the stairs and into his room where he carefully hid the box under some clothes at the back of his wardrobe.

2

Questions

For the rest of the day Asa wandered around in a daze. Nothing was normal, most of the shops in the nearby town of Mereton were shut and every other tree was on its side.

One shop that was still open was the camera shop so Asa dropped the film off to be developed. He could hardly wait to see the photos but only had enough money for the four-day service so had no choice.

Then he headed towards the library where he hoped to pick up a book on rare creatures that would explain the thing he'd found. But the library was closed – a horse chestnut had fallen on it and taken out most of the large-print section.

Everywhere he went Asa saw people merrily enjoying the catastrophe, sawing logs and hauling branches whilst recounting stories of horrible deaths across the county.

Asa wondered how long it would take to grow back all the trees.

He walked past the recreation ground and was pleased to find that his favourite fallen tree was still fallen and hadn't been blown upright in the storm.

But as Asa explored the devastated village his discovery was never far from his mind.

He resisted the urge to keep looking in the shoebox by staying out for the rest of the day but he made sure he was back before it started getting dark and the candles came out.

He ran up to his room but had hardly stepped through the door when he realised something was wrong. A rank smell hung in the air and as he opened the wardrobe he realised with horror that he had put the box right next to a hot-water pipe. The creature was still inside but it had changed. Instead of the limp body he had pulled from the pond the fairy was now stiff, frozen into a grotesque pose and its olive skin had turned grey. He briefly thought of freezing the creature before remembering that there was no electricity to power the freezer and by now the smell was so pungent he realised he would have to dispose of the body.

Twilight was drawing in so Asa lost no time. He opened his bedroom windows wide to let in some fresh air, took the box and set out on his bike the short distance to Cottingley Woods.

He knew the woods inside out having spent long, hot summers exploring every corner and climbing every tree. He cycled to a favourite spot where he sometimes made a campfire to cook sausages and there he started digging with a trowel brought from home. When the hole was deep enough he placed the entire box in and covered it over with soil. After that he scattered leaves on the patch to disguise it and sped off home.

That night Asa had a worrying thought. What if everybody knew about these creatures? Everybody except him? It was only a few years ago when his school friends had laughed at him because he still believed in Father Christmas. But what if this was the same situation but in reverse and he was the only one who *didn't* believe in fairies?

So the next day Asa tried to furtively ask questions that would determine whether this was the case. The trouble is that it is hard to find a subtle line of questioning on the subject of fairy-folk and he was unsure of the best approach.

Asa's mum sometimes used an expression when he was distracted or in a daydream, she would say he was 'away with the fairies'. Asa thought if he could get her to say it he could then quiz her about its origins. So, at breakfast he deliberately sat there looking gormless and staring into space, pretending not to hear when asked a question. But Mum wouldn't take the bait and after a while he felt a bit stupid so he just asked,

'Mum, what do you mean when you say I'm "away with the fairies"?'

'Well, you know, just that you seem to be in a different world, that you're playing with the fairies.'

'What fairies?'

'Pardon?'

'Which fairies do you mean?'

'*The* fairies, you know, *fairies*.'

This was less than useless so he decided to try his dad.

Dad was down the garden salvaging the wreck of the greenhouse. The hurricane had smashed five panes of glass and tried its best to make soup of the tomatoes. Dad, in his frustration, had decided to abandon this year's crop and try again next spring. He had dumped the bedraggled vines on the compost heap and was replacing the broken glass.

Asa asked him outright.

'Dad, do you believe in fairies?'

'Of course, son. Who do you think leaves you money when you lose a tooth?'

'Well, I know that's you. I know there's no *tooth* fairy. I mean other types.'

'Other types? What, like the one at the top of the Christmas tree?'

'That's an angel.'

'All right, smart-arse, go and do your homework.'

Later he found himself in the kitchen asking Mum:

'Why are fairy cakes called fairy cakes?'

'Because the fairies like them.'

'What fairies?'

'Please, Asa, don't ask stupid questions.'

But why was it a stupid question? Because everyone knew about fairies or because there was no such thing?

Either there was a massive conspiracy going on or he had made an earth-shattering discovery. Either way he was on his own.

3

Some Answers

Two days later the frustration was almost too much to bear. Asa was still no closer to explaining his discovery and at times he wondered whether it had all been a dream. There was still a whole day to go before his photographs were ready and at lunchtime Asa grabbed his bike and headed back to the woods.

What he found there filled him with horror. The patch where he had buried the body had been disturbed. More than that, the grave had been exhumed, and the shoebox and body were nowhere to be seen.

Asa started searching in the bracken but soon realised it was futile. Had an animal dug it up? A fox maybe? If so, where was the box? Could someone have taken it deliberately?

He raced back home to gather together all the loose change he could find. He needed answers. He had to see those photos.

As it turned out, the extra cash was not needed because the photographs were ready a day early. Or rather, the *photograph* was ready, as only a single, blurred print had come out.

The man in the shop was very sympathetic.

'How long have you had the film?' he asked.

'Don't know,' said Asa glumly, 'probably years, it's my dad's.'

'Well, that will be it, I'm afraid. Film doesn't last forever you see, it has a shelf life and after a while it starts to deteriorate.'

Asa looked at the print. At first he couldn't even make out what it was, it certainly wasn't the clear shot of the creature he had been hoping for.

Then he realised it was a very close-up shot of the tattoo on the creature's chest. It was out of focus but you could definitely make out the design. The shopkeeper craned his neck to see the photo.

'Hmm,' he said, 'like the one on the fairy. Don't worry, I won't charge you for that, I'm sorry you didn't get the rest of your prints.'

It took a few seconds to register what the man had said, but when it did it was like an electric shock.

'Pardon?' Asa coughed. 'What did you say?'

'Don't worry about the money, it's only the one print.'

'No, sorry, you said something about the photo.'

'Yes, that pattern,' the man pointed to the picture. 'It looks like the one on the fairy.'

He'd said it again! Asa couldn't believe his ears.

'What fairy?' he found himself asking.

'Not *fairy*, ferry. The Ferryman pub on Church Street has a plaque above the door with a similar design if I'm not very much mistaken.'

Asa expressed his gratitude as quickly as he could and set off for Church Street.

The street was full of modern shops and new buildings but halfway down was an old Tudor house whose upper floor jutted out over the pavement and whose roof sagged like a wet tarpaulin. This was the Ferryman and it had a painted sign above the door showing a cloaked figure punting passengers on a shallow boat. Asa thought this was odd as there was no river running through Mereton and it was ten miles from the nearest beach at Inglesea.

The man in the photo shop was right; above the door of the pub was a plaster plaque. Layers of paint had smoothed the outlines of the design but it could still be made out and it was the exact same pattern as the tattoo.

Asa stared at the plaque for a long while, trying to work out what it meant. Well, it looked as though it was old, and whoever had put it there must have known about the fairies. It just so happened that at the precise moment Asa was pondering the Ferryman, George, the town drunk, was being thrown out of it, laughing all the way. George spent his mornings in the pub, his lunchtimes being thrown out of the pub and his afternoons sitting by the war memorial with a can of strong lager and a couple of grubby friends. He was always good-natured, even when being thrown out of the pub and, as long as you caught him early enough, could hold down a half-decent conversation, or at least half a decent conversation.

Asa hurried over and offered a shoulder for the

old man to lean on. They shuffled over to a bench and George slumped down, giggling at a long-forgotten joke.

'How long have you been drinking in the Ferryman, George?' asked Asa.

'I only got there at eleven, and now they're throwing me on the street, thass what I'm saying,' slurred George.

'No, I mean how many years? Has it been a pub for years?'

'Used to belong to a madman, so they say, in the olden days.' George pulled a face and waggled his hands next to his ears in order to show what a madman might look like.

'Really?' said Asa. 'Who?'

''S the one what shot the birdie, the lil' birdie,' replied George.

Asa was confused.

'What birdie?'

'Stuffed the lil' birdie, didn' he? In the libree. Poor lil' birdie never hurt nobody.'

Suddenly George looked as though he might burst into tears. Asa gave him a pound for a cup of tea from the money he'd saved from the photos and that seemed to cheer him up again.

'The library, you say?'

''Sright, the lil' birdie in the libree.' George pointed in the general direction of the library.

'Thanks, George! I'll see you later.'

Asa headed off across town with a feeling he might know what the old man was talking about. In the entrance to the town library was a large wooden plinth and on it was a stuffed bird display under an old glass dome. The Mereton Warbler was a pretty songbird that had been discovered on Mereton Heath in 1780. That was the first and only time the Mereton Warbler had been spotted anywhere near Mereton but that didn't prevent it from being named after the town and becoming the town symbol.

4

The Mereton Warbler

The man who spotted the Mereton Warbler just happened to have a shotgun about his person at the time, as he was hunting hares. He shot the bird, had it stuffed and presented it to the museum under its present glass dome. Now, the Mereton Warbler was not a large bird so after the shot had passed through there was not much left for the taxidermist to work with. He made do with sparrow feathers, which he painted with watercolours, but a lot of it was presumably guesswork. The result was strange and a little creepy to say the least.

The corpse was crudely wired to a twig and at

its skull. Several powdery moths lay dead at the bottom of the display. A tarnished brass plaque on the base proudly declared the name of the murderer:

BENJAMIN TOOTH
ALCHEMIST INVENTOR
ASTRONOMER ASTROLOGER
SCIENTIST
7 CHURCH ST. MERETON
12TH APRIL 1780

The library, by this time, had reopened its doors although the large-print section was cordoned off with yellow tape saying DANGER – DO NOT CROSS in unusually big letters.

It was a familiar place to Asa, who had visited it every week for as long as he could remember and knew pretty much every book in the children's section.

There were two librarians, Mr Trap and Mrs

Fields, and the library was a very different place depending on who was working that day. Mr Trap was an irritating man who was probably quite young but dressed and behaved like someone much older. He had a moustache that didn't suit him, an air of weary resentment and a superiority complex.

He hated kids and if he could answer your question sarcastically, he would. But he treated the old-age pensioners with a cringey respect and talked to them about the weather and bus passes as if he wanted to be just like them. Asa found Mr Trap thoroughly nauseating and preferred the days when Mrs Fields was in charge.

Mrs Fields was the opposite of Trap. She was an old lady (genuine) with a friendly nature and a hearing problem. In fact she was so friendly and so hard of hearing that any job would have suited her better than a librarian. Readers were constantly asking her to 'shh' as she sang or talked to herself, unaware of the noise she was making.

Today was a 'Mrs Fields day' and there she was,

behind the counter, clumsily knocking over a stack of books with her elbow.

'Um, excuse me?' he said. Mrs Fields looked up and a big grin spread across her face.

'Hello, dear, how can I help you?' she yelled and a few people looked up from their browsing.

'Um, I want to find out about Benjamin Tooth, the man who shot the . . .'

'Benjamin Tooth!' Her grin spread wider and her voice got louder. 'Alchemist, inventor, astronomer, astrologer . . . !' She knew the brass nameplate by heart. A man in the Human Sciences section scowled and raised a finger to his lips.

'Shhh!'

'Sorry!' she shouted and then turned to Asa and giggled as though she had been told off.

'Follow me,' she whispered, and led Asa to the local history shelf. She took down a large book on the social history of their town.

'There will be something about him in here, dear.' Her voice was slowly rising in volume again. 'Look under his name in the index or under "Mereton Warbler" – he was the man who discovered it, you know.'

'Do you mind?' came a voice from the next aisle. 'People are trying to read.'

'Sorry!' called the librarian then she winked at Asa and scurried back to her desk.

Asa looked through the book and was quick to find a chapter on Tooth. It made interesting reading:

Benjamin Tooth was a familiar figure in Mereton at the end of the eighteenth century. An eccentric Jack of all trades, he dabbled in astrology, herbal medicine, botany and more. Seen by many as a con artist [and by a few as a devil worshipper], Tooth's main claim to fame is the discovery of the town's symbol, the Mereton Warbler. In later life he spectacularly fell from grace when, during the Napoleonic wars, a chimpanzee was washed up on the beach in Inglesea. He managed to convince the townsfolk that the ape was, in fact, a French spy and they arranged a trial at which it was found guilty of treason and thrown in prison. Before long word got out and the people of Mereton and Inglesea became the laughing stock of the whole country.

Because of this, Benjamin Tooth was mercilessly hounded by the townspeople until he eventually went to live in an old farmhouse on Windvale Moor. Though he kept the Church Street property and occasionally stayed there, most of his time was spent at his remote moorland retreat. There he continued his studies and would occasionally publish a scientific paper, copies of which he would then attempt to sell door to door. But after the chimpanzee incident nobody ever took him seriously again, and he even gained the nickname 'Fairy Man' after he started claiming to see elves and goblins on the moor.

Asa's heart leapt and he read on.

Many years after Benjamin Tooth had been forgotten by the townsfolk and the Church Street house had been turned into a tavern, a huge trunk was found on the steps of the library and with it, the stuffed Warbler under its glass bell. A note explained that the trunk contained the entire body of Benjamin

Tooth's life's work that was to be donated to the people of Mereton even though they had ill-treated him all those years ago. Unfortunately, whoever left the items forgot to leave a key for the heavily locked trunk and, because of its great weight, it stayed where it was left for many years. The mounted bird can still be seen on display in the library entrance but the whereabouts of the trunk has long been forgotten.

Asa slapped the book shut and stood up, then he sat down again, found the chapter and read it through for a second time just to make sure. Then he slapped the book shut and stood up again. He looked briefly around him as if he expected to see the trunk sitting, forgotten in a corner gathering dust. It wasn't, so he wondered what to do next. The first thing to do, he thought, is to have a good think about what to do next. So he set out to find somewhere a bit quieter than the library, somewhere he could concentrate.

As he walked home he sifted through the information he had just unearthed and thought about what it all meant. Most importantly, he knew he was not insane, and neither was Benjamin Tooth. Tooth was the only other person that knew about the fairies; the problem was he lived nearly two hundred years ago and, for that reason, was unavailable for a chat. Asa's hopes rested on a locked trunk that had also been missing for almost two centuries. What were his chances of finding it? Where could it be?

But he was almost certain he knew where to find the elves or goblins or whatever they were. Benjamin Tooth, so the book had said, lived on Windvale Moor, a wild, rugged area twenty miles from Mereton. The wind was blowing from that direction on the night the storm brought the creature into his garden. Windvale Moor was the place to look.

5

Windvale Moor

The next day was a Tuesday and again Asa was free to do as he pleased. The previous night he had meticulously planned his trip to the moor, writing lists of equipment and provisions and secretly gathering everything together. At first light he crept downstairs, scribbled a feeble lie on a piece of paper explaining to his parents where he hadn't gone, slipped out the back door and cycled off towards the south-west.

As the sun rose and the morning started warming up the ride was a pleasant one and the town petered out around him, replaced by farmland. This in turn became sparser until, coming over the brow of a hill a little over two hours later, Asa saw the huge expanse of Windvale Moor stretching out before him.

The moor seemed so vast at first that it made Asa feel dizzy. It fell away from him in a turbulent shaggy carpet of grasses and furze, then rose up another sweeping hill and away again on to the horizon. Through the bottom of this valley wound a narrow, fast-flowing stream. He felt like a tiny dot on the landscape but at the same time, very conspicuous, as though he were being watched.

He stood in that one spot for a long time, just trying to get a sense of scale. He could hardly focus his eyes and felt as though, if he were to take a step on to the moor, he would be swallowed up. He took out his binoculars and spent some time watching a small herd of deer on a faraway hill, which helped bring things into perspective.

Eventually he set off down the hill and stopped at the stream. There were no reeds or vegetation along the banks of the brook, the grass just ended as if a machine had cut the channel, but the water

was crystal clear and sped over smooth pebbles. Asa spotted small brown trout swimming against the current and rising to snap at flies.

He tasted the water, which was sweet and pure, and then carried on up the other side of the valley until he reached an overhanging bank where he sat down and took out his binoculars again. He stayed for an hour in this position scanning the valley below him for signs of life. As his eye became trained he started to pick out small birds in the vegetation, reed warblers and yellowhammers flitting from perch to perch, tiny brown or blue butterflies blown across the grass and pockets of grazing rabbits. But no fairies, so he continued over the hill and into a more rugged terrain with rocky outcrops and wind-stunted trees scattered across the heath.

He found another sheltered position and settled down again to watch and wait. Far away across the moor he spotted a distant farmhouse and he wondered for a moment if this could be the remains of Benjamin Tooth's isolated home.

Just then his attention was grabbed by a bird of prey that crossed his view and soared along the ridge of a hill.

The hobby, like a miniature peregrine falcon, skimmed above the waving grass before catching a thermal and rising a few metres, hanging in mid-air and scanning the ground for prey. Then it dipped its wings and dropped out of the current to swoop away and make another low pass above the heather. Asa had been watching the falcon's nimble aerobatics for ten minutes when it suddenly dived behind a patch of heather and out of sight. It reappeared almost immediately, hovered above the spot and then plunged down again. Now Asa saw what it was chasing, as something scooted out from under the bushes and darted away. The hobby saw it and once again lunged with talons outstretched. The prey leaped clear into the air and hung there for the briefest of seconds allowing Asa a glimpse of what looked like a huge dragonfly.

But the bird would not give up and was soon

upon it, lashing out and sending it spinning to the ground. Asa leaped up and in an instant was tripping and stumbling down the hill, waving his arms and shouting for all he was worth. He was over a hundred yards away but had not gone further than a few steps before the hobby spotted him and took off across the moor. Not long after, Asa arrived at the spot and collapsed to his knees panting for breath. He hadn't seen whether the bird had escaped with its prey and searched the grass around him.

Just then he heard a buzzing noise in the gorse, like a bluebottle trapped in curtains. Asa stayed on his knees and slowly approached the bush. The buzzing stopped, and then started again, and he inched closer. Something was caught in the shrub, trying to get out, but he couldn't get a clear view. He saw something move towards the top of the bush, it buzzed briefly, dropped and was silent. Asa leaned in and pushed the lower branches aside – a shape had got caught in the thorny twigs and buzzed frantically in panic. Asa reached towards it, parting the leaves and saw what the hobby had been after.

It was unmistakably the same type of creature he had found in his garden, with the huge eyes and long limbs, but this one was very much alive. Asa looked it directly in the eye, and saw in its face an expression of shock and confusion. One of its wings was tangled in the thorns and as it pulled to get free it seemed to scream in pain though it made no sound. Asa extended a hand towards it that made the creature struggle even more violently until the wing tore and it darted out of reach. It flew up and away but immediately tumbled back into the long grass, the torn wing impeding its flight. It reappeared and seemed to find some strength as it flew some way before plummeting again out of sight. Asa glimpsed it a couple more times as it flitted away, zigzagging into the distance.

He looked again in the gorse and found a shimmering triangle of wing snagged on the thorns. He carefully removed the shred and flattened it out on his hand. He wondered if it would grow back. The speed at which the thing had moved, even with an injured wing, was incredible and Asa realised that a butterfly net would be useless if he wanted to catch one. The only reason he had got so close this time, indeed the only reason he saw it at all, was because the hobby had spotted it first.

As he got to his feet and started making his way back to his bike he thought about the missing trunk containing Tooth's studies. How much had

Tooth discovered? Had he managed to catch a live specimen? Maybe he had even befriended them. Asa had to find that trunk.

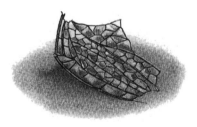

6

An Accident

The next day Asa could hardly move his legs. The forty-mile bike ride had caught up with him and he hobbled around like a geriatric. He couldn't bear to sit on his bike so he caught the bus into town and painfully limped the last stretch to the library.

It was a Trap day. Inside he waited for the surly librarian to finish stamping somebody's books and then he stepped up feeling like Oliver Twist about to ask for 'more'.

'I need to find the chest of Benjamin Tooth,' he announced.

Trap looked blankly at him.

'Benjamin Tooth,' offered Asa, 'the man who shot the . . .'

'I know who Benjamin Tooth was,' said the librarian.

'I need to find his trunk.'

'You mean the trunk containing all his works?'

'Yes.'

'The one that has been missing for two hundred years?'

'Yes.'

'Certainly, if you wait here I'll go and get it for you . . .' and he turned to go.

Asa could not believe his ears.

As it turned out, he was right not to believe them for Mr Trap was being sarcastic and turned back with a withering look.

'Oh, I'm afraid the *lost* trunk of Benjamin Tooth is still *lost* at present.'

'Have you looked in the cellar?'

'No.'

'It's probably in a dark corner where it's been forgotten. In the cellar.'

'Really?'

'Yes, can't you go and look? Or I could go?'

Mr Trap regarded him incredulously.

'No, I can't, and neither can you.' Even though this wasn't strictly sarcasm he said it in a sarcastic way and turned to stamp the next person's books. Asa knew he would get nowhere with Mr Trap so thanked him sarcastically for his help and went to leave.

What occurred next seemed to happen in slow motion. As Asa left the reading room and went to walk out of the building his shoe slipped on the marble floor. Clumsily trying to regain his balance he fell against the wooden pedestal and gave an almighty, flat-handed shove to the Mereton Warbler display case, which slid away from him and disappeared over the edge. Then came the unmistakable sound of two-hundred-year-old town history smashing on marble floor. Asa peered over the plinth at the disaster.

The wooden base had split in two, the glass dome had split into a hundred and seventy three, and the bird itself (which, after all these years, was only held together with dust and air) had all but disintegrated. It was nothing more than a small mound of fluff and fibres. But there, on the ground in amongst the bits of dry feather, was a key on a long silver chain. Without thinking or hesitating Asa scooped it up and dropped it into his coat pocket just as the doors burst open and all hell broke loose.

There followed lots of questions like: 'What were you doing?' and 'Whatever were you thinking of?' and sometimes 'What do you think you were playing at?' Questions he couldn't possibly answer because they didn't mean anything, and anyway, the fact was, he didn't feel bad about what had happened, how could he? It was meant to happen. Benjamin Tooth had hidden the key in the bird for the person who was clever enough to find it. Or the person who was stupid enough to fall over and discover it by accident.

Asa did a good job of pretending to be sorry about the incident and found himself agreeing to help out at the library, unpaid, for the rest of the week.

This was perfect as far as he was concerned; if the trunk was still in existence it would most likely be in the library, where it was left. If it was as big and cumbersome as the book had described then the furthest they would have taken it would be the library basement. It had to be down there, and Asa's 'community service' was the ideal way of gaining access.

7

Search for the Chest

The next morning Asa turned up at the library to find Mr Trap in charge again. As he got to know him a bit better Asa found that Mr Trap wasn't as annoying as he had first thought. He was far worse – and kept adding to the reasons not to like him. One of those reasons was the endless mugs of tea that he drank. Not normal tea but some foul herbal concoction that smelled like stewed bathmats. Asa overheard him telling an old, uninterested gentleman that the tea helped his blood pressure.

Asa soon discovered that there were really only

two jobs to do in the library: stamping outgoing books, and putting the incoming ones back on the shelves. Mr Trap, obviously, did the stamping (it gave him a feeling of power) which left Asa to replace the returns. It was a mindless, repetitive task but Asa didn't really care, he quite liked mindless, repetitive tasks, they allowed him to think about other things. Right now, for example, he was trying to think of a way or an excuse to get down to the library basement.

Just before lunch Asa came across a large cardboard box of old and damaged books so he took them to Mr Trap.

'Shall I take these down to the cellar?' he asked as innocently as he could manage. Trap looked over his bifocal glasses.

'They're to be thrown away,' he said.

Asa was surprised. 'Thrown away?'

'Yes. That's right. Thrown away,' Mr Trap said, speaking to Asa as if to an imbecile.

'But I didn't think old books got thrown away.

I thought they got stored somewhere. Like in the cellar.'

Mr Trap stepped up the sarcasm.

'Exactly which *cellar* are you referring to?'

'The cellar? The basement where you keep the books?'

'We tend to keep the books on the shelves so that people can read them.'

'You mean there isn't a basement storeroom?'

'No.'

'"No" that's not what you meant? Or "no" there isn't a cellar?'

'"No" there isn't a cellar.'

'I don't believe you.'

The librarian nearly spat out his tea.

'You don't believe me?' he spluttered, unable to think of anything sarcastic to say.

'There must be a basement or something! All old buildings have a basement.'

Trap made a wide, sweeping gesture with his hand. 'If you can find one, you can help yourself to all the treasure you find therein. But please try not to disturb the other readers.'

Asa spent the rest of the day replacing books on shelves with the silver key nestled in his pocket. He secretly tried it in any lock or keyhole he found but without much hope and without any results.

He was stumped, the library cellar, he now realised, had been his only idea. With two more days of his punishment to serve and the biology field trip starting the day after it did not look like he would get any time to himself for a while.

But the very next morning as he left the house Asa intercepted the postman and took the mail from him. Amongst the other letters was one addressed to his parents that he instantly recognised as being from school. There were no outward signs but he knew the envelopes they used and the strange sense of foreboding that accompanied them. He opened the letter on the way into town and was delighted to read that there would be no classes for another week as essential repair work was carried out and that, as such, all school trips were postponed until further notice, including Asa's biology field trip.

Mrs Fields was back at the library, which was a breath of fresh air not least because she didn't drink smelly tea. She, as always, was very up for talking and soon confirmed what Asa hoped Mr Trap had been lying about; that there was no cellar under the library building.

He decided to tell the old lady the truth about wanting to find the trunk and asked her if she had any ideas where it might be.

'I don't think it's still around, dear,' she said looking sorry, 'unless they have it locked away somewhere in the council building. But Benjamin Tooth was seen as a madman so I think they probably disposed of it not long after it was left.'

Well, that's that, thought Asa and reluctantly accepted that the lost trunk was well and truly lost.

8

Discovery

The next day Asa's legs were recovered enough to cycle into town but he met Mrs Fields getting off the bus and walked the last bit with her.

'I tried to phone you last night,' she said, 'but the phone lines were down again.'

'What about?' he asked.

'About something the workmen found after you left yesterday, something I think you will be interested in. With the Mereton Warbler display gone there was no use for the wooden plinth it stood on so we decided to get rid of it to make more space in the entrance. Well, it seems the pedestal is fixed into the floor. It seems it was constructed on the spot . . . around something. They think there's something hidden inside it.'

'What do you mean "think"? Didn't they find out?'

'Well, it was closing time so they're coming back this morning to have another look.'

By then Asa and Mrs Fields were approaching the library and he ran ahead and up the steps into the entrance hall. There was the wooden plinth in position but one of the side panels had been prised open at the top and now there was a gap of about an inch along one edge. Asa looked in. Too dark. He was pulling at the panel as Mrs Fields arrived and scolded him, telling him to wait until the workmen got here, before he broke something else.

But the workmen didn't arrive for hours and Asa couldn't concentrate on anything because he was in no doubt as to what was hidden in the cabinet.

And, he was right. When the builders eventually

turned up they did so with crowbars and made short work of the rest of the plinth revealing what was undoubtedly the lost trunk of Benjamin Tooth. But Asa had never imagined it to look like this. The chest was massive, presumably made from wood but covered in riveted metal plates; a sort of homemade armour plating and on the front was a hefty iron padlock. It was so heavy and cumbersome that instead of moving it they had eventually built a box around the trunk and used it to stand the Mereton Warbler on.

Asa squeezed the key in his pocket so hard that, had it been confiscated, he could have taken an impression of it from his hand.

There was no decoration on the chest save for two tiny letters stamped into one of the metal plates. Mrs Fields leaned in to take a look.

'B.T.,' she read.

'British Telecom?' said someone stupid.

'No – Benjamin Tooth!' she exclaimed. 'It's the lost works of Benjamin Tooth!'

* * *

All morning people buzzed around the trunk and poked things into the keyhole until Mr Trap turned up and cordoned it off with the large-print tape.

It was arranged that a locksmith would come at lunchtime to open the chest and, with him, a photographer from the local paper to record the event. Mr Trap was in his element running around making phone calls and notifying people of what he started referring to as 'my discovery'. Asa suspected he was going to try and get in the photo come lunchtime.

By one o'clock word had spread enough that a small group of twenty or so people had gathered in the library atrium to see the chest opened. The photographer took a few shots of the trunk with the broken-open pedestal and then the locksmith knelt down beside it and set to work with a selection of thin, pokey tools. Everyone held their breath. Eventually they all had to let that breath go and take another one, which they held. But it soon became apparent that this might take some time and before long everyone was breathing normally again.

The locksmith's ears and cheeks started to go red as he worked under pressure. He shook his head and tutted. Trap leaned in with a furrowed brow as if he might be able to spot the problem.

The photographer lowered his camera and said, 'Can't you do it?'

It's what everyone was thinking but it didn't go down well with the locksmith, who snapped, 'I need to concentrate, and you're standing in the light!'

The photographer wasn't standing in the light, he was nowhere near, but he took a step back anyway and adjusted his focus.

Ten minutes later and the small crowd were starting to drift away when Mr Trap, who had been to answer the telephone, burst back into the atrium and held up his hands triumphantly.

'Hold everything!' he announced, which seemed odd, as nothing had happened for ages.

He paused dramatically and continued, 'I have just got off the phone to the BBC,' another good pause for reaction, 'who asked me if they can send a television crew, here, to the library, and film the opening of the chest live on tomorrow's breakfast news!' With that he looked as if he wanted to take a bow but instead just took a dainty step back and awaited the applause he so obviously thought he deserved. The applause was not forthcoming and as people started to leave he called after them, 'Tell all your friends! Let's get a good crowd here tomorrow, shall we?'

Nobody answered but the locksmith remarked, 'I don't know how you're going to get this open on live TV, I can't shift it.'

'It's all right,' said Trap, 'I know a man with bolt cutters.'

Asa had to think of a plan quickly. He had a day to get into the trunk, but when would he ever get time alone? Only after the library was closed and the building was locked. The only way would be to hide somewhere in the library and spend the night there. There was still enough of lunchtime left to speedily cycle home and grab some provisions. A torch and spare batteries, some sandwiches and a bottle of water. It's never good to lie to your parents except perhaps when you are on the brink of an earth-shattering discovery so Asa left a note to say he was spending the night at his friend Chris's house and he wrote down the telephone number. This was a confidence trick as his mum already had the number but if it was written down for her she would be less likely to check. Asa would just have to hope she didn't.

The first part of the afternoon was spent looking for a likely hiding place until Asa suddenly realised that both the outer doors and the inner doors to the reading room would be locked. This meant he would have to actually be hiding in the atrium when the building was locked. The atrium, of course, was completely bare apart from the locked trunk and the empty pedestal that used to cover it. The pedestal! It was easily big enough to get inside and if he pulled it flat against the wall once he was in it would be impossible to know he was there.

The rest of the afternoon dragged painfully slowly and Asa kept drifting into the atrium to look at the trunk and the box, wanting to get in to try it for size. When five o'clock eventually came around and everyone had left, Asa got his bag from behind the counter and bid Mr Trap goodbye as nonchalantly as he could manage. Then he walked into the atrium and with a glance behind him ducked down into the wooden pedestal. Once inside he got hold of the edge and tugged the box against the wall and there he sat, hardly daring to move, waiting for the librarian to leave.

There was space inside the box but not enough to stretch out fully and it soon started to become uncomfortable. When finally, after half an hour, Mr Trap left for home, he locked the doors behind him without noticing a thing.

Once he had gone Asa pushed the box with his shoulder until there was a large enough gap for his feet to stick out and he could lie down flat. He stayed that way, in the box with his bag as a pillow, and listened to the footsteps of people outside walking back from work until, eventually, he drifted off to sleep.

9

Tooth's Works

It was dark outside when he was awoken by voices coming up the library steps. It took a few seconds to remember where he was but when he did he pulled his feet sharply back inside the box and listened. It was the group of teenagers who usually hung out by the clock tower. They reached the door and peered in at the trunk but Asa could not make out what they were saying. At one point they rattled the locked doors and he thought they might break in but after another ten minutes they got bored and moved off.

Asa waited until all was quiet outside and then

heaved the box away from the wall.

Slowly and painfully he inched his way out. It felt so good to be free that he just lay on his back on the marble floor for a few minutes looking up at the ceiling. It was dark in the library but the orange glow from the street lamps outside threw just enough light to see by.

Asa pulled himself up on to his knees. His instinct was to keep low in case anyone passing saw a shadowy figure in the library and called the police. When there were no cars it was insanely quiet but the echoey entrance hall amplified any noises that Asa made. His nerves were fraught as he approached the trunk that was sitting solidly where it had been left two centuries before. Taking the silver key from his pocket he pushed it into the padlock and turned it once. But rather than the clunk of a latch opening, it made the ratchet sound of a clock being wound. A mechanical click sounded from somewhere inside the lid of the trunk and then a low whirring began. Asa waited, the whirring faded and then stopped. Silence. He tried to lift the lid but it still wouldn't budge. He took the key again, thought, here goes, and began to wind. Immediately he could hear things starting to happen inside and after ten or twelve turns the key would turn no further. Deep within the box musical notes began to faintly chime a ghostly tune and a shiver ran up Asa's spine. The tune came to an end and as the last chord hung in the air there was a dull clunk-click; the trunk seemed to sigh, like someone loosening their belt after a big dinner, and the lid slowly raised a couple of inches.

In the streetlight's glare he could see that the sheer volume of papers in the trunk had pushed the lid up when the lock was released and a few loose leaves slipped silently to the floor. The smell of the paper was almost overwhelming. The same dust-and-old-paper smell that you'll find in any library but so concentrated he could almost taste it. If you squeezed the chest you could probably extract pure essential oil-of-library.

There was not enough light to read by so Asa took out the torch he had brought and turned it on. Suddenly the entrance was flooded with light and he hurriedly clapped a hand over the beam. He sat in silence for a while and raised his head enough to peak out of the window. The street outside was deserted and so, allowing just a sliver of light to escape between his fingers, he tentatively examined a page.

The handwriting was spidery, scratched into the paper in a manic frenzy with blots and splatters around every word like a cloud of gnats. Asa studied it closely but couldn't make out a single word. It wasn't that it was illegible but it seemed to be written in a different alphabet. He spent a few minutes trying to decipher the scribbles before noticing that most of the sentences started with a full stop. It was written backwards! He looked around for a reflective surface but the only thing was the window out on to the street. He ducked down low and crawled over to the double doors. Then, squatting awkwardly, he tried raising himself just enough to see the reflection of the page in the window but this didn't work as it was too dark. After a few further experiments Asa found if he shone the torchlight through the paper from underneath he could just make out the backwards writing. Try as he might he could not stop wild shadows dancing on the walls whenever he moved the torch and so, with an armful of papers and ledgers to sift through, he crawled back into the wooden pedestal, where the light would be hidden, and set to work.

Most of the pages were written on both sides, which made it confusing as he skimmed through the documents for anything of interest.

The pages seemed to be in no particular order, starting halfway through a sentence with no headings or titles, and the writings just appeared to be the ramblings of a madman:

. . . this 16th day of August did receive from Mr Weighbury the sum of 8d. for a pot-hook and a peck of prunes. The latter, he said, were to calm his bilious winds whereupon I offered him my bladderwort and arum tonic. But, I fear Mr Weighbury must have been drunk for no sooner had he swallowed a beaker or two but he came violently ill and began writhing on the floor in a most embarrassing fashion.

I sent him on his way having charged him a ha'penny for the medicine.

*

. . . only product of which was a foul-smelling grease, which I have yet to find a use for.

*

. . . pound for pound apples are worth the same as horses . . .

. . . and flung the entire pudding, in its bowl, across the paddock and into the dyke, a distance of some fifty-seven yards. The pudding was sadly ruined by ditch water but the bowl had miraculously stayed in one piece.

For the next few hours Asa sat inside the wooden pedestal shining the torch through the pages and searching for some sort of lead. When he had gone through a pile he would emerge, lie on his back, stretch his limbs, and then get a new pile of documents to go through.

The pages at the top of the trunk seemed to have been thrown in as an afterthought and the further he dug down the more ordered the documents became with projects bound into ledgers, dated journals and some printed material that was written the right way around. There were also lots of maps, graphs and diagrams, detailed watercolours of plants and animals. Asa felt he was close, but could still spot nothing relating specifically to the fairies.

The town clock chimed every hour but nonetheless Asa had lost all track of time. Did I just hear the clock? Was that three or four o'clock? Did I fall asleep? The spidery writing was becoming harder and harder to focus on and his head began to pound.

Reaching the end of a particularly big stack of papers he was shocked to count seven chimes of the town clock and he peeked out of his box to see the sky outside beginning to lighten. He had an hour, hour and a half at most, before Mr Trap came to open up. There was one more hefty armful to go through and as there was now more light he spread the sheets out on the marble floor. He had given up trying to read the words and was now just scanning the drawings and paintings. That's when he came to a large leather-bound book with two straps and buckles that held it shut. He undid the buckles and opened the book to find that it was, in fact, a box with a hinged lid, the inside of which was a mirror. Inside the box was a roll of parchments tied with a black ribbon and two smaller leather-bound volumes, the first of which had a title scorched on to the front. Asa lifted the book, held it to the mirror and read the title:

The Windvale Sprites

This was it! He had found it. He didn't even bother to open the book but put it back into the mirrored box with the roll of paper and shut the lid. He placed the box in his hiding place and started to load the rest of the work back into the trunk. Without the box there was extra space in the trunk and as he pushed the lid closed the mechanisms whirled back into action and the trunk locked itself shut.

Asa squeezed back into the box and waited for somebody to come and open up. Then a ghastly thought occurred to him. Today was Sunday! The library was closed all day! But just as a panic was starting to rise Asa heard the unmistakable sound of Mr Trap's irritating footsteps approaching the library steps and he remembered the television broadcast and breathed a sigh of relief. He heard Trap cross the entrance looking for the key to the reading room, then he stopped and all went quiet for a moment, as if he had spotted something. Asa held his breath and could hear his own heart pumping in his chest. Mr Trap took a large breath in through his nose seeming to notice the strong, musty smell of the papers. But he obviously thought no more of it and let himself into the reading room, switching on lights as he went. Asa looked out and, through the window in the inner door, watched until Mr Trap went into the staffroom to prepare the first of many cups of foul-smelling 'tea'. Then Asa slipped out of the front door with the large package under his arm and made his way home in an excited daze.

10

The Windvale Sprites

Mum and Dad were up and packing for their trip and were surprised to see Asa back so early from his sleepover.

'Oh yes,' said Asa, thinking on his feet, 'Chris's family all go to church on a Sunday.'

'Do they?' said Mum, surprised. 'Well, I never would have guessed.'

She was eyeing the box under Asa's arm.

'And I wanted to get back and read these comics that Chris gave me,' answered Asa before she had a chance to ask. She sniffed the air.

'What are they? They smell old.'

'Yes,' said Asa, again making it up on the spot, 'they're Chris's grandfather's comics . . . Space Dan and the . . . Space . . . Rockets . . .'

'Right . . .' said Mum, and he was able to slip past and up the stairs.

Back in his room Asa took out the box and carefully removed the first of the leather-bound volumes, opening it on the first page. He set the mirrored box on the carpet, sat cross-legged in front of it, and began to read:

I have discovered a colony of creatures on the Moor that I believe are new to science. At first glance they are insects: giant dragonflies; but on closer inspection appear to own human characteristics though I have yet to capture a specimen living or dead. I have spied them thrice at a distance and then only fleetingly.

The clearest view was that of a pair who were tussling or playing. No sooner had I spotted them but they somehow became aware of me and looked about as if they sensed they were under observation. Whether they saw or smelled me I know not but they were gone in the direction away from me in a flash. All three sightings were within a mile stretch of the river course, on the south-facing banks of the downs. I shall return next week to this spot.

The first few entries in the journal did not throw up much more new evidence. Tooth's next few trips were failures followed by a few more fleeting glimpses.

Asa took the roll of parchments and carefully unfurled it to discover a series of hand-drawn maps of Windvale Moor. These were marked with different coloured symbols indicating

Tooth's sightings and observations. The maps also confirmed that the building he had spotted on his trip to the moor was indeed Benjamin Tooth's old farmhouse as he had suspected.

Turning back to the journal Asa came to a chapter entitled:

On experiments in trapping techniques

From the diagrams it was clear to him that Benjamin Tooth had no regard for the lives of the sprites, just as he had none for the Mereton Warbler. The first ideas he tried were rabbit- and bird-catching methods: wire snares and miniature sprung metal traps, but these had apparently been unsuccessful, at least in catching sprites:

> . . . the trouble being that I do not yet know what the beasts feed on. Those spring traps I baited with honey remained set,

those I laced with flying ants catch'd
meadow pipits. No matter, I shall dine on
pipit pudding and ponder.

The experiments got steadily crueller, incorporating barbed hooks and sharp blades, wire nets and pits of broken glass but nothing seemed to work and Tooth's writing got scratchier and angrier.

But whatever he tried next must have worked because when Asa turned the page he was presented with a beautifully detailed watercolour painting.

For some reason this was almost better proof to Asa than the body in the pond or even the live ones he saw on the moor. Those already seemed like distant memories but here was hard evidence that somebody else had seen them too and Asa studied the picture closely for a long time.

The creature in the painting appeared to be older than the ones Asa had seen. Its skin looked darker and more weathered and the thorns running in seams up its arm and legs were much longer. It

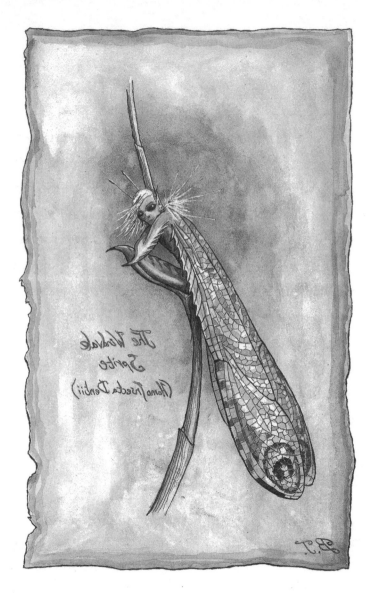

The Winged
Sprite
(Homo Insecta Zohlii)

seemed to be clinging on to the stem of a plant with its wings folded down its back towards the artist. They were the same dragonfly wings as Asa had seen but much more brightly coloured with a large 'eye' like a peacock feather at the tip. But though it was beautiful, there was something in the creature's eyes that disturbed Asa.

He turned to the next page of text and began to read in the mirror:

At last! I have captured a live specimen! The people of Mereton will rue the day they ever hounded me from their stinking town. I shall be rich!

First things first: to give the beast a name. Pending a thorough internal examination I have provisionally classified it as a new species of the homo genus displaying characteristics of the 'Odonata' order of insects. Therefore it shall be called 'Homo Insecta Dentii' (the latter for myself) but it shall be known as The Windvale Sprite.

The trapping method that eluded me for so long was, as is often the case, so simple as to be laughable. I soon found from my observations that there are two things the creatures cannot resist:

1: Any crack or crevice, ditch or dyke they can't help but explore. (They live, from all I can gather, in old warrens that the rabbits have either abandoned or been chased from, as I was from Mereton.)

2: (And this is the thunderbolt!) Shiny things! Be it a new penny or a shard of broken glass, if it reflects the sun they want it and will go to any lengths to get it.

My discovery was made thus:

Two days ago, whilst keeping my heathside
watch I happened to drift to sleep in the
afternoon sun. I was presently awoken by
a buzzing sound and on stirring surprised
two of the creatures who made off with
great haste across the moor. I looked down
to discover three of my silver coat buttons
gone, the thread bitten through. Stolen!
It was only then that I thought back and
remembered other items mysteriously
vanished: a shoe buckle, a watch chain and
my amber hatpin. All no doubt pilfered
by those winged rapscallions.

But they are sly! Or clever, for when
the traps were obvious they stayed away,
sensing danger and anything mechanical
or sprung they would steer clear of.

And the solution was a bucket. A mere bucket from my yard, baited with a silver sixpence, sunk into the ground with a heavy lid propped up on a stick that I pulled away on a twine.

The first two attempts brought them close but they sensed or smelled me and fled. Working on the theory that they have an extraordinary sense of smell, on the third attempt I endeavoured not to touch any of the components of the trap with my hands and wrapped my feet in wads of grass lest my footprints should carry my scent.

And that was the key! I waited 'til it was inside and tweaked the twine from my position downwind. The lid came down and the prize was mine.

The following pages had more sketches of the creature from different angles and detailed drawings of its wings and limbs. But in every one the sprite seemed to be trying to hide with that same frightened look in its eyes.

11

Back to the Moor

'Asa!' Mum was calling from downstairs so Asa hurriedly swept the books and papers under his bed and leaned over the banisters.

'Yes?'

'What time are you off?' asked Mum.

'Off where?'

'Don't tell me you've forgotten? The school trip, your biology field trip, it's today, isn't it?'

Asa *had* forgotten, or at least he'd forgotten to tell his parents that it was cancelled. But just at that moment a plan occurred to him: with Mum and Dad away at his grandparents' he would be free to go and spend some time on the moor trying to catch a sprite.

'Ah yes,' he replied, 'we've got to be at school at midday.'

'Well, we're leaving soon,' she said. 'We can give you a lift with all your stuff.' Asa thought fast. 'It's OK, Chris's mum is picking me up on the way past.'

His mum seemed to be satisfied with this fictional arrangement and so he went down and kissed her goodbye before going back to his room.

He spent a few hours meticulously planning his expedition like a great explorer of old. He drew up lists of provisions and spread Tooth's maps and charts on the floor. Some of them showed smaller areas of the moor in greater detail and marked out entire colonies of sprites and the locations of their warrens. The maps were, of course, two hundred years old but Asa thought that even if the colonies had moved on the moor it would give him an idea of the sort of terrain the creatures preferred.

The day before the storm Asa's dad had taken him to get all the things he would need for the school trip and they had remained packed in his new rucksack at the end of the bed. He checked everything and repacked the bag. He had a brand-new tent (unfortunately it was bright yellow but Asa had some camouflage ideas), an ingenious tin spirit stove which all packed away inside a small saucepan, a sleeping bag and a roll-mat. To this he added his binoculars and the maps of the moor. Clothes, Asa decided, were not a priority so he packed as little as possible but made sure he had enough waterproofs. The remaining space in the rucksack he packed with food supplies raided from the kitchen: a few cans, dried noodles, cereal bars. He envisaged being hungry by the time he got home but he didn't have the space to carry more.

Next he went about collecting the bits he needed for the trap according to the instructions in the book. So as not to leave fingerprints that the sprites might smell he wore some old gardening gloves to pick up a tin bucket which he tied on to the side of his bike. He found a trowel and various lengths of twine in the shed and a spool of fishing wire that he put inside. Then he selected three large old sweet jars in which he hoped to put his captured specimens.

With everything secured he hauled the rucksack on to his bag and wheeled the bike out on to the pavement.

He soon realised, as he struggled to keep the bike upright, that this time the journey would take a lot longer than two hours. On long, flat stretches he could get up to a relatively good speed but as soon as there was the slightest incline he had to dismount and walk. As he pushed the laden bike up one of these hills with the jars and buckets clanking he imagined he looked like Benjamin Tooth returning to his farmhouse after an unsuccessful trip to town to sell his potions.

The journey to Windvale took him most of the day. Not only did he have a heavy load but now

he felt the need to hide in the bushes at the side of the road every time a car came by. It was quite conceivable that a friend of his parents could be driving past and recognise him, and he did look slightly conspicuous, like a travelling tinker.

The journey took the rest of the afternoon and the shadows were beginning to lengthen when Asa eventually arrived on the edge of the Moor. The bike was now a hindrance as he could not cycle across the long grass and so he left it well hidden under a rocky bank. With the bucket and jars slung about him Asa now resembled some kind of one-man band as he set out on to the moor. The rucksack was heavy and he soon decided to look for a likely base camp so that he could dump most of the weight. He headed north towards the stretch of river where Tooth had sighted the sprites most frequently. He came to a point where the ground fell steeply away below a long ridge that sheltered numerous crags and hollows. Asa found one, not quite deep enough to be called a cave but it was well sheltered from the wind and there was room to pitch his tent. Once it was up he tied bunches of grass and reeds to the outside until it looked like a part of the landscape and he put his rucksack inside.

He sat down in front of the tent and spent an hour scanning the landscape through his binoculars. Birds and insects went about their business in the long grass but no sign of the hobby and no sprites.

Before too long his eyes started to droop and, though it was still early evening, the previous night's lack of sleep and the exhausting journey there was taking its toll. He crawled into his sleeping bag and lay for a while listening to the strange silence of the moor. The wind ruffled the tent and he heard the occasional shriek of a barn owl but before very long he was fast asleep.

12

Tooth's House

It took Asa a few minutes to figure out where he was when he opened his eyes. The yellow light in the tent was unfamiliar and he lay there for a while trying to remember.

Emerging slowly, he blinked in the sunlight and looked around. The air was chilly and the grass was damp with dew but the sky was clear and cloudless with the promise of a beautiful autumn day.

He set up his little stove and heated water for a cup of tea, warmed a tin of vegetable soup and as he ate he thought about the day ahead. The first thing he wanted to do was take a closer look at

Benjamin Tooth's farmhouse. He didn't expect to find anything there but as it was a definite, stone-built part of the story it seemed a good place to start.

He cleared away the stove, zipped up the tent, slung his sack over his shoulder and set out.

As he approached Asa was again overcome by that self-conscious feeling of being watched.

The house was a solid, stone building with a slate roof and, though it had done well to stand up to the ravages of time, the moor was slowly reclaiming it. Grass sprouted between the roof tiles giving it the appearance of a balding thatched cottage and the walls were covered with creepers. At one end a tree had grown up inside the house and burst through the roof where the wind made the branches grow horizontally. An ornate but broken weathervane on a crumbling chimney made the whole place look like a crackpot mechanical device that had been abandoned on the moor. It all fitted in with the description of Tooth and his weird lifestyle.

The front of the house had the look of a stern face frowning down at him and a shiver ran up Asa's spine. Reaching the edge of what was once a garden surrounding the house he hesitated. The perimeter drystone wall had melted over the years to a long, shallow mound of flat rocks, completely covered in places by a blanket of turf. He picked his way over the boulders and rusty iron railings and made his way towards the entrance.

The front door to the farmhouse was solid wood and, though the rest of the house was crumbling, with windows and shutters hanging from their hinges, the door was locked and impassable.

Asa made his way around the side to where he found a low window with cracked green glass. It was dark inside, but Asa could just make out the shapes of furniture and tattered drapes hanging from the walls.

Around the side he found a small outhouse with a door at the back which led into the main building. This outhouse was filled with old tools

and what was once a small handcart that had long since separated into its individual components. A jumble of twisted iron parts Asa discovered were animal traps rusted into a solid, tangled mass like a deadly tumbleweed and next to it a pile of wooden half-barrels and buckets. He nervously stepped over the junk towards the door which was open a crack and he peered through. There seemed at first to be music coming from within but he soon realised it was just the wind whistling through holes in the house like a church organ. He pushed the door – it didn't budge. Either the hinges had rusted solid or there was something behind it, so Asa gave a hard shove. The door creaked and splintered and went crashing to the floor, whipping up a dense cloud of dust and cobwebs. With a new channel to escape by the wind rushed out, blowing dust into Asa's face. He stumbled blindly back into the junk, sneezing and rubbing his stinging eyes.

Once recovered he gingerly took a few steps into the house.

What he found inside was weird. It was obvious that the remote building hadn't had a visitor for two hundred years. Instead of the empty rooms and broken furniture that Asa had expected, he found the rooms filled with stuff, piles of it, all covered with a thick layer of dust. He shone the torch around. Mouldy books and stacks of paper, bizarre scientific instruments and rows of bottles and jars covered every surface. It looked as though it had been used as some sort of laboratory.

There were threadbare rugs on the floor, moth-eaten hangings on the walls and, on a solid oak table by a window, a bottle of wine and a glass, the contents of which had long since evaporated leaving a dark residue. It was creepy, abandoned in a hurry like the *Mary Celeste*, and so caked in grime that anything he touched stirred up a cloud of dust. To search through everything would have taken weeks and Asa didn't quite know what he was looking for – anyway, he had the information he needed in the journals. If anything, this discovery was just confirming what Asa already suspected, that Benjamin Tooth was a madman, and an unpleasant one at that.

He was about to head back to the moor when something on a dresser caught his eye. It was a small model of a tricycle intricately made from twisted wire and sitting on a wooden base. Closer inspection revealed it to be not so much a model but a working miniature with pedals and a chain that, though now rusted, had once worked like a real tricycle. Tiny straps, perished strips of leather, had once been attached to the saddle, pedals and handlebars and as he studied it Asa came to realise with horror what it was for. It was exactly the right size for one of the sprites to ride but only after it had been tied to the contraption.

Asa wondered what the 'scientist' had been up to, as if the discovery of a new species on the moor was not enough, it seemed as though Tooth had been intent on getting the creatures to perform tricks. This idea, along with the overpowering smell of mould and damp made Asa feel slightly sick and he carefully made his way back outside into the sunshine and fresh air. He knew all he wanted to know about Benjamin Tooth and decided he didn't much like the man.

The rest of the day Asa spent searching for the sprites in vain. He poked around in countless rabbit holes looking for signs of life but to no avail and if it were not for his earlier encounter he might possibly have given up hope. But he knew they were here and he was determined to find them. As the shadows once again started to lengthen at the end of the day he decided to set the bucket trap anyway by an old warren not far from the tent.

Wearing the gloves, he wedged the bucket into a rabbit hole, placed one shiny coin in the bottom and scattered a few more on the grass around it. Then he put one of Mum's chopping boards over the bucket, propping up one edge on a twig to which he tied the end of the fishing wire. Then he made his way back to the tent, unwinding the wire as he went.

Once in his shelter he lay down on his front and watched the trap through the binoculars, holding tight to the trip wire, until it got too dark to see.

13

Capture

He awoke at first light with his head still outside the tent and dew on his hair and eyelashes. He found he was still gripping the fishing wire in his fist but looking through the binoculars he could see that the lid of the trap was still propped up on the twig.

He set up the spirit stove and cooked some eggs and bacon, which he ate in the chilly morning air as the moor started to wake around him and birds emerged from who-knows-where to chase midges.

He decided to set his trap at a likely looking place he had seen by the stream near some old rabbit holes. But as he rewound the fishing wire he realised with a start that the coins were gone. None on the ground and none in the bucket. He searched in the grass for a short while but was convinced they had been taken, and taken by something nimble enough to get into the bucket and out again without disturbing the trap.

He looked around him. Were they watching him? He *felt* as though he was being watched but, then again, he often did.

He decided to reset the trap in the same position; the wind was blowing back towards the tent, which would disguise his smell. He fished in his pockets for two more coins, placed one in the bucket, one on the grass, and retraced his steps, unravelling the line as he went.

Back at the tent he heaped more grass and branches on the flysheet until not a scrap of the yellow fabric was showing, and settled down to watch.

Hours rolled into each other and before long Asa

had lost all track of time. The moor was buffeted by winds and there were fewer birds and insects than the previous day. Occasionally he spotted the hobby negotiating the gusts of wind and watched intently, but when it dived down it reappeared empty-taloned.

The excitement at finding the coins gone slowly waned throughout the day so that by early afternoon Asa found himself nodding off and had to pinch his arm to stay awake. This worked for a while but inevitably he was soon asleep and stayed that way for a couple of hours.

When he awoke the low sun was shining in his eyes and he squeezed them shut again and enjoyed the warmth on his face. It was then that he became aware of something moving close by, a rustling in the grass to his left. With amazing self-control he managed not to sit up and look or even open his eyes but remained still and listened to the noises. Whatever was there seemed to be furtively looking around his camp and checking out his stuff. Then, a fluttering, buzzing sound and a shadow crossed his face and disappeared. Asa continued to lie stock-still until he was sure it had gone and then, as slowly as he could manage, he turned his head and squinted out across the valley.

Even without binoculars he could see that the trap was still set. But then, with a rush of excitement, he spotted them. Sprites, two of them, hiding in the shadow of the overhanging rock not five yards from the bucket trap. They were huddled close together but as he watched, one of them flitted out from its cover, hovered over the trap and then zipped back again. They're checking it out, thought Asa. They looked smaller than the other two he had seen, maybe they were young ones, and maybe they were more adventurous or foolhardy, because Asa was sure that they knew he was there and that the bucket was some sort of trap. A moment later one of the sprites rose several feet into the air and hovered, seeming to look back across the valley towards him.

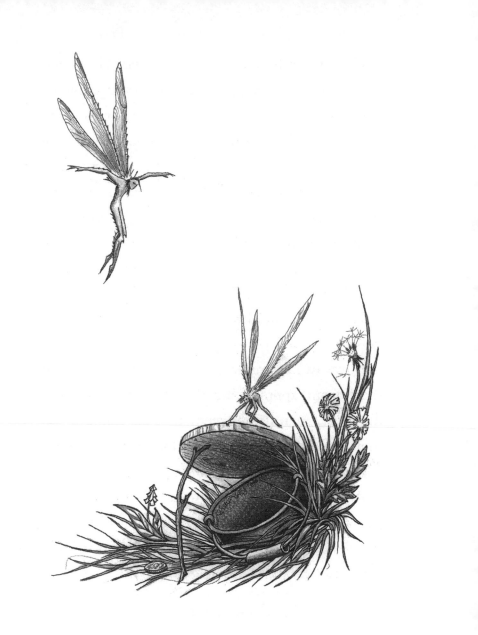

He stayed motionless and pretended to be asleep until the creature dropped back down and joined its mate. For ten minutes Asa hardly dared to breathe as the two sprites continued to nervously dart close to the bucket and then back into the shadows, into the air and then back under cover. Each time one approached the trap it got a bit closer while the other stayed high and kept watch. Eventually one of them, in a lightning move almost too quick to see, dipped down and scooped the coin from the ground before they both disappeared into the long grass.

It was twenty minutes or so before Asa spotted them again, approaching the site from a different direction. Again they seemed to be building up their confidence, one edging close while the other kept watch.

Asa felt the fishing wire in his hand, which he had tied around his wrist to save losing it. He realised that he would have a split second to react when the creatures made their move, and if he messed it up he would not get another chance.

Suddenly something in the sprites' movement told him they were ready. Very deliberately one of them rose high into the air, hung there for a second and, with an acrobatic flip, seemed to signal the all-clear. The second sprite whipped from its hiding place and straight into the bucket. Asa reacted as if given an electric shock, he leapt to his feet, hauled the fishing line back over his head and, without waiting to see if it had worked, started racing down the hill.

As he ran he could see a flurry of movement around the bucket. One of the sprites circled it frantically, trying to lift the fallen lid. Tripping and stumbling as he ran Asa found himself shouting 'Hey! Hey! Hey!' and waving his arms. He saw the second sprite look up and flit this way and that in a confused panic. It pulled at the side of the bucket, it whisked into the air and down again, it threw itself against the lid and scratched at the wood. Asa was only a dozen strides away when it turned and looked briefly towards him, whirled around and was gone.

Asa stopped a few feet short of the bucket and sank to his knees gasping for breath. Excitement and exertion beat in his chest and ears and he felt so weak he thought he would pass out. He tried to calm down. Pull yourself together, he told himself and counted to ten or twenty or however long it took to come to his senses.

He edged forward on his knees towards the sprung trap. From within the bucket came the sound of an angry swarm of bees whipping around and Asa knew he had his prize.

Not quite knowing what to do next he found himself laying his hands flat on the lid and saying 'Shhh'. Instantly the creature inside was silenced. Asa bent his ear close. Inside the bucket the terrified creature seemed to be listening just as intently.

He started to slide the lid back, a millimetre at a time until a thin crescent of daylight shone into the pale. He peered in close but it was still too dark to see. Maybe the sprite was under the lid. Ever so carefully he pushed it back further and the gap got bigger. Then, without warning the sprite bolted out through the crack and into Asa's face. He fell back with a cry and threw his hands up grabbing hold of the creature as it batted about, clinging to his nose, blinded by the sunlight. He cupped his hands around it and pulled it away from his face. The transparent wings stuck out the top of his fist and buzzed wildly whilst its body writhed and wriggled in his fingers. He almost had it safely back in the bucket when he felt a stabbing pain in his right hand so sudden and intense that he heard a whistling in his ears. Despite this he managed to plunge the creature into the pail and slide the lid back across before succumbing to the pain. He rolled around on the grass, squeezing his hand and repeating 'ow, ow, ow, ow', which seemed to help a little until the ringing in his ears subsided and he dared to look at his wound.

In the middle of his right palm was a minuscule fleck of blood atop a tiny raised bump, not the gaping flesh wound he had been expecting, and he soon realised that he had been stung rather than bitten. His hand was throbbing and, not knowing how poisonous the sting might be, he decided to get moving.

Most, if not all, of his stuff could stay hidden on the moor. There was no need to take the tent and stove home if he was going to be coming back soon to collect more specimens. Using the fishing wire he made sure the lid was securely tied to the bucket and he pulled the whole thing out of the rabbit hole. He then gripped the bucket in front of him with both arms and started walking back across the valley to the tent. The sprite was alternately still and silent or manically buzzing as Asa negotiated the bumpy ground.

He packed the tent quickly and rolled up the sleeping bag, stuffed everything else into the bag and pushed the lot way back under a craggy rock.

Then he piled more rocks in front and on top of the bundle until it was well hidden. So well, in fact, that Asa took a few minutes to remember some landmarks and features so that he would find the spot on his return. Then, gripping the bucket tightly, he started back to his bike and from there, the slightly wobbly cycle home.

14

Tooth's Cruelty

By the time he got home it must have been half past nine and, with Mum and Dad not yet back from visiting his grandparents, the house was silent and dark.

He dumped his stuff in the house and then took the bucket with the sprite out to the garage. Dad proudly called it a 'tandem' garage, that is, it had space for two cars parked end to end. They had never owned more than one car though and the back end of the garage rapidly filled up with 'things to take to the dump'. In here was Asa's old guinea-pig hutch where he intended to house the sprite for the night. It was a large cage with a strong wire-mesh front and separate sleeping compartment at one end.

He placed the entire bucket in the hutch, closed the front and then, poking a bamboo cane through the wire mesh he pushed the lid off the bucket.

At first there was no movement and Asa began to worry that the creature had not survived the journey. But suddenly and without warning it shot out and batted about wildly inside the hutch for a few seconds before disappearing into the sleeping quarters out of sight.

Asa returned indoors and went to his room where he pulled out the second of Tooth's leather-bound journals.

On the first page a painting of the moor in all its wild and rugged beauty. Scrawled at the side in Tooth's spidery writing was a poem:

Oh! Ancient sea
This Windvale moor
A palette for the world
Where pestle sun in mortar sky
The seasons' pigments grind and mix,
'Neath grey and blue
And thinned with dew
Where gale and gust the colours blend
Nor'easter wind the knife to send
And spread them o'er the earth

The verse surprised Asa who imagined Tooth far too self-obsessed to spend time being poetic. Perhaps there was a sensitive side to the old rogue after all.

But as he read on those hopes slowly began to fade.

After his first successful capture it seemed Tooth had no trouble trapping further specimens and as Asa turned the pages he saw numerous drawings of them, male and female, young and old.

Notes and observations were scribbled all around the pictures. One in particular got Asa's attention, an arrow pointed to the sprite's foot:

All are equipped with a vicious sting, as I have experienced many times to the detriment of my poor nerves. A barbed thorn at the base of the ankle administers the venom, which is painful but lasts no longer than a bee sting. The animal can twist its body wildly though, and sting even when you think you have a good grip on it. These days I wear leather falconry gauntlets whenever I handle them.

Asa wished he'd at least read that bit before he'd gone to the moor.

On the next page was the heading:

A Note on Housing and Feeding

This was the information Asa was most keen to find out so he eagerly read on:

The creatures are best housed in small birdcages of the type used for finches. No cover need be provided as this encourages them to hide and makes observation impossible. They prefer to cling to a vertical branch rather than a horizontal perch but their wings are best displayed when the cage is left bare and they must cling to the bars.

A water bowl may be provided but one need not offer food, as the creatures will not feed in captivity.

And that was it. Benjamin Tooth was only
concerned with making a name for himself by
discovering a new species and being hailed a great
scientist. He simply was not interested in the
welfare of the sprites or probably even keeping
the creatures alive. The facing page had a pencil
illustration of a frightened sprite clinging to the
inside of an ornate canary cage. It was a stark
image compared to the watercolours but the next
piece of writing confirmed his fears:

A Note on Pickling and Preserving:

Though I continue to try to keep one of the creatures alive for a period they rarely last three or four days before their refusal to eat and their self-harming tendency makes them useless for experimentation. Therefore it makes sense to kill the specimens as shortly after capture as possible so as to preserve them in a prime physical state.

They can be dried and pinned out as one would a large insect. I have achieved this a number of times but the body shrivels somewhat and loses shape as it dehydrates. Also the skin darkens in colour.

Salting does not work as the exoskeleton is impervious to salts and the insides continue to decompose.

Pickling is the best of a bad selection until I find some better method. A solution of formaldehyde, water and methanol in a half-gallon jar will keep a specimen indefinitely but all colours fade to a uniform yellow-grey within a matter of weeks.

Each gruesome description was accompanied by an equally grizzly illustration; twisted bodies in glass jars, wizened specimens stretched out and pinned on boards. It was hard to tell how many of the things Tooth had killed; he probably lost count himself. The reading got worse still as the scientist started dissecting his specimens and sketching the internal organs and bones.

All of this helped Asa decide that he would approach his studies from a different angle, as a conservationist. He would concentrate on the areas Tooth did not, on how the creatures lived,

what they ate, and how they could be protected.

It was getting late so Asa closed the book, resolving to build the sprite a proper spacious home first thing in the morning.

He got into bed and closed his eyes but for a long time his brain was swimming with the sinister images of pickled sprites in half-gallon jars.

15

The Greenhouse

Next morning he set to work early.

Straight away he knew he wanted the sprite to have enough room to fly around and, remembering how last summer a starling had got trapped in the greenhouse, he decided to see if it could be made into a suitable home.

At the end of the garden, obscured from the view of the kitchen window by a holly hedge, the recently repaired greenhouse was ideal.

He started by fixing netting over the windows at the top so they could be opened to let in fresh air. Back in the garage he unscrewed the legs of the hutch and, by putting it on his skateboard, was able to wheel it relatively smoothly down the garden. He placed it on the ground in the corner of the greenhouse and taking a spade and wheelbarrow he proceeded to pile earth and compost on top, leaving the entrance clear. Down by the pond he pulled great handfuls of long grass which came up with a wad of roots which he planted all over the mound until it started to resemble a burrow in a grassy bank.

Asa then carried the broken remains of Dad's tomato vines back into the greenhouse and tried to untangle them. Those that could be saved he replanted in pots and the snapped stems he hung up at the glass to provide shade and cover. He wedged some branches high up for perches and by the end of two hours he had created a nice little habitat that looked a lot more appealing than a birdcage. He made sure the greenhouse door was slid shut and then carefully reached in and pulled open the front of the guinea-pig hutch.

All was quiet and still from inside and Asa withdrew to the opposite corner of the greenhouse and watched like a statue. He didn't have to wait for long before he heard a faint shuffling and saw a shape edging to the front of the box. Suddenly the sprite shot out of the hutch and flew vertically upwards, slamming into the roof. It fell down, momentarily dazed but then zipped across, ricocheting off the glass. Asa threw up his hands, wanting to stop it, wanting to catch it and prevent it hurting itself, but that only terrified the creature more and it became even more frantic.

Deciding that recapturing it would be impossible, Asa lowered his arms and stood very still. Then he slowly started to lower himself down so that he was sitting in the corner clasping his knees. The sprite, dazed and exhausted, slowed a bit. It hid in the tomato vines, watching Asa and catching its breath before again attacking the glass in three or four places. It soon learned that the panes were solid but was clearly confused by it, touching the glass with its fingertips and pushing with its shoulder. All the while it kept an eye on Asa who sat as still as stone in the corner.

Asa watched as it searched for a means of escape but after about ten minutes it disappeared back into the hutch and didn't come out.

He slowly got to his feet, sneaked out of the greenhouse and set about thinking what the sprite might like to eat.

In the kitchen he chopped soft fruit into small pieces – grapes, banana, tomatoes – and poured some honey into a saucer. He gathered a large vase of flowers from the garden, ones that insects seemed particularly to like and even found a few caterpillars, which he put in a jar. Returning to the greenhouse he laid the offerings on the ground in front of the mound and settled again in the far corner to read some more of Tooth's journal.

16

Destruction

For the next two days Asa spent most of his time in the greenhouse. The sprite eventually became less nervous and would venture out of the hutch and fly up to perch in the tomato vines from where it would watch him reading. But it never got closer than that and it never showed any interest in the food or water he had brought.

Benjamin Tooth, in his writing, was starting to show signs that he was quite as mad as the people of Mereton had suspected all those years ago.

He had become convinced that the tattoo the sprites wore on their chests held some sort of

mystical secret and that whatever it represented had the power to grant a long life:

1st July

Those that bear the markings appear to be older than those without and several seem to be of a very great age indeed. I have counted the growth ridges on the exoskeleton of a particular individual and calculated it to be at least a hundred and fifty years old.

He started concentrating his efforts on one colony that inhabited a large abandoned rabbit warren about a mile from his house:

All of the marked specimens I have collected came from the vicinity of this nest so I conclude that the answer to the mystery will be found there.

I have started digging on the south-facing bank. It is hard work and I could use some help but I'll be damned if I shall share this discovery with even the lowliest labourer.

Tooth went on to describe how the sprites would periodically attempt to mount an attack, swarming him and stinging any exposed skin until he was forced to cover up completely and wear a beekeeper's hat as he dug. But even this didn't appear to deter them:

4th July

I have been stung by the spiteful little beasts one too many times, and have lost all sympathy for, and patience with them. Tomorrow I will go to town and purchase some ferrets with which to drive them from their burrows. Then I can continue to excavate without risk of being constantly stung.

The ferret plan worked as well as I could have wished. After securing nets across every hole I could locate I sent down the two animals who were eager and hungry. Almost immediately the sprites started to flee and were trapped: I netted a dozen good specimens of varying ages. Unfortunately I seem to have missed a hole on the northern side of the warren and soon witnessed a mass exodus of perhaps a hundred individuals who flew in a swarm away across the moor to the north-west. A breakaway group must have doubled back, however, and I was stung severely several times on the buttocks as I tried to coax the ferrets back out.

Once they were gone I lost no time and began to dig.

The entrance tunnels are extraordinarily deep and only after two hours' solid work did I come across a first 'room'. A small dugout containing nothing but a pile of acorn cups. A stockroom perhaps? There are no oaks on the moor so they must have been gathered from far afield, perhaps used for bowls or drinking vessels. I progressed another couple of feet downwards before the tunnel started to level out to horizontal. It started to get dark and though I was tempted to return to the house and get candles to work through the night, the wind was starting to pick up and the clouds threatened rain. I barricaded the hole securely before I left with stones and rubble to prevent the creatures returning to their home and stealing any of their possessions back.

A further three or four feet along the passageway I fancy it starts to open up into a much bigger chamber. I shall return at daybreak on the morrow.

Asa went to bed that night with a heavy heart. Reading about Tooth's decimation of the colony made him feel that he was a part of the ruthless plan. Though he had endeavoured to provide a comfortable environment for his specimen the sprite was still not eating and was spending more and more time hidden from view in the burrow.

His parents were coming back in two days and he resolved that if there was no change by the end of tomorrow he would take the creature back to its home.

17

The Statue

The next morning Asa let himself into the greenhouse and froze. The sprite was lying motionless at the entrance to the burrow, its rich olive-coloured skin now a pallid grey.

But as he closed the greenhouse door the creature looked up and pulled itself back out of sight.

Asa knew he had to take it back to the moor.

There were only a few pages of the journal left to read and, though he didn't expect the story to end happily, he was curious to know what Tooth had discovered.

6th July

I have found it! The object that the creatures hold in such high esteem and which I am certain has some kind of mystic power of eternal youth. It is mine!

I'll be brief as I have many dissections to perform on the captured specimens and they are dropping like flies.

When I returned to the warren at first light there was indeed some evidence that a group of them had been back to salvage their treasures but the rubble barricades were too much for them. They had started to dig new tunnels down but they had been abandoned, probably as they saw me arriving.

It didn't take long to reach the room I mentioned yesterday, some sort of dining hall with earthen tables and benches in rows. Other rooms and antechambers lead off of this hall, dormitories perhaps, but nothing of great interest was found here.

It was then that I realised the fresh tunnels that had appeared overnight were on the other side of the mound. Whatever they were so desperate to retrieve was obviously on that side. I started to dig in the direction of these new holes. After an hour's hard graft the ground suddenly caved in and revealed a large chamber filled with objects, the collected treasures of generations of sprites. They were the shiny trinkets that I have come to know the beasts cannot resist. Lots of junk and scrap metal, spoons, nails, stained glass, and my stolen coat buttons and hatpin, all polished to a high sheen. But amongst the rubbish are many valuable items, numerous coins, some of them gold, dating back to Roman times, small pieces of jewellery and gems. I shall spend many enjoyable evenings sifting though my hoard, grading and valuing the treasure.

The floor of this grand 'hall' (though it is, in actual fact, no bigger than the size of my pantry) had semicircular earthen ridges radiating out from a central point, presumably seating, and at the centre was the object of my search. A figure, a totem fashioned in wood, perhaps rose or holly, barely eight inches tall and exactly as represented in the tattoos the creatures bear which have intrigued me so greatly. It is a beautiful piece of work with carving so intricate it can only have been rendered by tiny hands but, more than that, as soon as I grasped it and tore it from its base I felt an invigorating wave of health and vitality pass through me. The aches and cramps of the previous day's exertion evaporated and I felt as strong as an ox.

This wild place, this unforgiving Windvale Moor that I have come to love has finally rewarded me.

A possible plan is to grind the statue to a fine powder and use it in potions that will guarantee long life and health. This I will sell at great profit, not to ordinary people but to Kings and Queens, only the very rich, and then so shall I be. It cannot fail.

Asa turned the page to a beautiful painting of the object (whatever else you could say about Benjamin Tooth, he was a skilled artist).

The sculpture was a carved statue of a young sprite squatting on top of a grotesque, six-legged creature with a long tail that curled underneath to form a base.

Asa could recognise in it the shape of the pond-sprite's stylised tattoo but this carving was exquisitely detailed. The wings of the sprite showed every vein and even the thorns on its limbs were there.

It reminded Asa of a dragonfly hatching from a nymph.

As he studied the page he suddenly got the feeling that someone was looking over his shoulder. Thinking it was his mum or dad he slammed the book shut and wheeled around. With a frantic, panicked buzz of wings the sprite, which had somehow crept from the burrow and around behind him, zipped upwards and crashed into the glass.

Stunned, it dropped again, spun around twice and then darted back inside the burrow.

Asa crept slowly over to the entrance and, clearing the plates of untouched food to one side, he opened the book at the painting and laid it on the ground. Then he retreated to the door and watched. Ten minutes passed, twenty, but then, after half an hour, he thought he saw a movement from within. Sure enough the creature, crawling on all fours, came nervously into view and crouched at the opening. It was watching him. Asa crossed his arms on his knees and laid his head on his arms to show that he was not about to pounce or attack it.

The creature spread its wings and buzzed up into the air, hovering above the book looking down at the picture. Then it turned to Asa and looked at him with an expression of pain and questioning. It slowly held out its long, willowy arms towards him and then dropped on to the page and ran its hands over the painting.

'I don't have it,' said Asa. 'I don't know where it is.'

The sprite again reached out its hands as if it were pleading with him.

'I don't know where it is,' he repeated. 'The old man took it.'

With a flick the sprite's wings became a blur and it rose slowly into the air. It drifted forward until it was floating no more than a foot from Asa's face. It filled his vision and he was suddenly aware of nothing else but this incredible thing in front of him. He could see, in magnified detail, every hair on its head, its filament fingers, the hundred glittering surfaces of each hypnotic eye. From somewhere distant he heard an echoing, ringing note and then a word.

Help.

Nothing had been said out loud, the word had been planted without a voice in his brain.

Help.

Asa said nothing but found himself replying: *How?*

Help us.

I want to.

The creature pointed away.

Home.

A great sadness washed over Asa as he looked deep into the sprite's eyes.

'OK,' he said. 'I'll take you home.'

18

Home

Asa didn't need any further supplies for this trip. He simply wanted to return the sprite to the moor. Suddenly the whole adventure seemed like a mistake. He was as bad as Benjamin Tooth. What right had he to steal one of these rare creatures from its home and keep it captive? He knew what he had to do: set the sprite free, leave them in peace and never whisper a word about them to another living soul.

He placed his open rucksack on the ground and pointed to it. 'You go in there,' he said. 'You ride in the bag.' He stepped back and the sprite flitted over to inspect it. It looked at the bag from all angles then settled on top. It dropped inside and then shot out again, circled round and once again came to rest on the bag. It looked at Asa and seemed to be happy enough with the arrangement.

Asa put the bag on his back as the sprite hovered nearby.

'You get in there,' he said, gesturing over his shoulder, but it took no notice.

'OK, well, it's there if you need it,' and he stepped out of the greenhouse to fetch his bike.

The sprite seemed to understand the plan and regained some of its former energy and colour. It was constantly on the move, darting into bushes and up into the trees, zipping through Asa's legs and circling above him.

He wheeled his bike out of the back gate and around to the street. At the first sound of a car the sprite was straight in the backpack and remained there until he was well away from busy roads and human habitation. But as soon as the roads turned into lanes and the town became fields and countryside it emerged again.

The sprite seemed fascinated by Asa's bicycle, hovering close by and watching the wheels spin, marvelling at the unlikely contraption. Sometimes it flew on ahead and other times it stayed close by. Occasionally it would perch on his shoulder and he could feel the breeze of its wings beating next to his ear. Various times when the road meandered off course the sprite would fly off across a field and be waiting for him on the other side.

He knows the way, thought Asa, so why does he even need me to come? But then whenever a potential danger showed itself, a passing tractor or a large bird overhead, the sprite would seek the safety of the bag and stay there until the danger had passed.

When eventually they came to the moor and Asa could take his bike no further, he laid it on the ground and stood for a while to catch his breath.

'There you go.' He gestured to the wide expanse
of waving grasses. 'Home.'

The sprite hung in the air in front of him.

'You're home,' repeated Asa. 'This is where I
found you, I don't know *exactly* where you came
from.'

The tiny creature darted away for several feet
but then stopped and turned again to face him.

'What?' Asa asked. 'I don't understand.'

The sprite flew in close and hovered right in front of his face.

Come.

The word hung in his head as if it had been placed there. Asa knew he was supposed to follow.

The sprite then started leading him down the grassy slope and across the moor. Sometimes it was ahead, sometimes behind like a sheepdog shepherding its herd.

But it soon dawned on Asa that they were heading towards Benjamin Tooth's broken-down house and he hesitated. He remembered the macabre scenes of dereliction and decay and did not want the sprite to see Tooth's instruments of torture.

'No, wait,' he called out to the sprite who was quite a way ahead. 'Why are we going there?'

He was suddenly aware of a movement to his left and, looking down, he saw another sprite in the grass peering at them. Then a whispering rustle made him look behind and there were three more, and then another, and soon the tiny creatures were all around. They rose up on shimmering wings from the sea of grass and hung there, watching.

Looking back, the sprite was waiting for him. It had a plan and so he followed.

When they got to the house the creature's mood changed. It no longer led him but hung back and seemed to be urging him on. The sprite could have entered the house through any one of the broken windowpanes or holes in the roof but for the first time it seemed to want to stay close to Asa and be protected by him.

He picked his way over the ramshackle remains of the garden and towards the outhouse where he had entered before. The sprite grew more nervous as they approached and clung on to the back of his head, peering through his hair. As he stepped over the rusty junk the sprite gripped his head tightly.

'Are you sure?' asked Asa.

Go on, said the words in his head and so he continued into the dark interior.

Once inside they stopped and the sprite, little by little, started to look about the room.

It was cloudier today than when Asa had visited before and only the ghostly outlines of furniture could be made out by the dim light that came through the grimy windowpanes.

'I don't have my torch,' said Asa. The sprite settled on the thick stub of a candle, folded its wings around, and, with a sharp, rasping, scratching sound, leapt back as the ancient wick flared up and settled into a steady flame. Asa took up the candle and followed the sprite.

It seemed to be searching for something amongst all the junk. It was momentarily fascinated by the wire tricycle and studied it closely, looking back at Asa as if to say, 'This is like yours.'

'I know,' said Asa. 'It was made for you.'

The sprite pointed through the door into the next room where Asa had not previously ventured and so together they pushed on into the unknown.

The door opened out into what would have been the hallway of the house with the remnants of a large staircase leading to the upper storey. The whole of one side of the staircase had collapsed and the remaining timbers were so rotten it would have been impossible to climb. The sprite made a circuit of the hallway and then disappeared under the stairs through one of the gaping holes. Asa picked his way carefully over the broken banister railings and peered into the dark space. He couldn't see a thing but could hear the buzz of wings coming from down below and he realised there must be a cellar underneath the house.

The sprite soon reappeared and seemed to be keen for Asa to follow him down. He made his way over more rotten planks towards the back of the hallway where, in the gloom, he could just make out a small doorway.

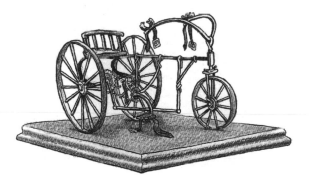

19

An Ancient Find

The door creaked open on rusty hinges and Asa pushed the candle ahead of him to reveal a stone staircase leading down into the gloom. As he gingerly made his way down, the sprite hovered close by. At the bottom of the steps was a large cellar that was filled with bookcases arranged in rows like a library. Boxes and chests took up almost every inch of floor space and everything was draped in thick cobwebs. Whatever the sprite was searching for it would be like finding a needle in a haystack.

The only clear space was a path down the centre

of the room between the cases and, with his heart pounding, Asa inched his way slowly forward.

As he passed each bookcase he peered into the spaces between them. Some of the shelves had collapsed and the leather-bound tomes were strewn over the floor and on top of yet more boxes. The candle spat and spluttered and sent shadows racing up to the ceiling as his footsteps tapped on the flagstone floor. But then his footsteps fell silent. He looked down and saw that the ground appeared to be covered in a dusty grey rug of some sort. He crouched down to take a closer look. No, it wasn't a carpet but more like wool or hair spread out across the floor, and up ahead it appeared to get thicker and deeper as if a pile of the stuff had been dumped at the end of the room behind the last bookcase.

He took another few steps. Something was not right. The sprite gripped his shoulder. Not wishing to go any further but resisting the urge to turn on his heels and run, Asa leaned forward and peered around the last set of shelves. What he saw was a truly bizarre thing. It did indeed appear to be a large mound of whitish wool piled up in the corner but perched on top of it was a small triangular hat.

Asa looked at the sprite who was staring at the strange sight with an expression of terror.

'What is it?' Asa's voice, though barely a whisper, echoed in the silence of the cellar as though he had shouted. Something beneath the pile began to move. Expecting a nest of rats to come scurrying out, Asa took three steps back and watched. The pile of hair settled again but Asa's hasty retreat had stirred up a cloud of dust and he could feel a sneeze brewing. He tried his best to suppress it but the more he did the more powerful it became until it burst from him, the loudest sneeze he had ever produced.

'HATISHOOO!' he exploded. The mound of hair heaved and shifted and the sprite, in a flurry of wings, disappeared back from where they had come. All Asa wanted to do was follow it out of there but his legs had turned to stone and he couldn't move an inch.

'Who's there?' demanded a raspy voice from somewhere inside the heap of hair. It was all Asa could do to stop himself collapsing in a dead faint.

'Who's there?' it repeated. 'What time is it?'

Asa held his breath.

'Is that the baker's boy? How long have I been asleep?'

Filled with horror, Asa watched as a bony hand with long, curling fingernails emerged from the white hair and reached up to push back the tricorn hat. Then it slowly parted the hair underneath to reveal a tiny pair of wire-rimmed spectacles sitting on a thin nose.

'Who are you?' croaked the voice.

'Asa,' he managed to squeak.

'What?'

'Asa Brown.'

'Are you the baker's boy? What time is it?'

'Not sure, about half past four I think.'

'Then you're late,' it said. The skeletal hand proceeded to remove the glasses and a pair of beady eyes glared out as if from behind dusty curtains. 'Well,' it eventually snapped, 'have you brought my loaves?'

'Um, I'm not from the bakery,' said Asa.

'What day is it?'

'Friday, no, Saturday.'

'Well, which is it, boy?'

'Saturday.'

'Curses! I only meant to have a nap!' The skinny hand replaced the spectacles and disappeared back inside the hair. The pile heaved and shifted as the old man tried to haul himself to his feet. But before long he gave up and slumped back.

'What's the month, boy?'

'October,' replied Asa.

'Confound it!' he shouted 'I've missed my birthday!' Then the mound of hair leaned slowly forward.

'Who is the present monarch?'

'Queen Elizabeth the Second,' said Asa.

The hair pile gasped and wheezed.

'Great Scott!' it yelped. 'It's worked! I'm still alive! I am immortal. Do you know who I am, boy?'

'Are you . . .' Asa stammered, 'are you Benjamin Tooth?'

'Indeed I am!' he shouted triumphantly. 'And you, boy, are trespassing on my property for which I am going to give you the thrashing of your life!'

Once again the old man tried to pull himself to his feet but once again he soon gave up.

'Come here!' he shouted. 'So that I can thrash you!'

Asa, of course, was not about to step forward for 'the thrashing of his life' and replied, 'No, I won't.'

Tooth thought about this.

'Very well,' he eventually said. 'Why can I not stand up?'

'I think it's the weight of your hair and beard, sir,' offered Asa. For the first time Tooth looked down at himself.

'Odds bodikins!' he burst out. 'Look at me!' (Asa had been doing nothing else since the ill-fated sneeze.) 'I must have been asleep for a hundred years!'

'I think it's more like two hundred, sir.'

'Gadzooks!' Tooth spat. 'Fetch me my razor, boy, I must shave this thing off.'

'No,' said Asa.

'Why the devil not?'

'Because then you'll give me "the thrashing of my life", sir.'

The old man took a second to process this reply and then the hair-pile started to gently shake. At first Asa thought he was quaking with rage but soon realised the dusty heap was silently laughing.

'Clever lad,' he said. 'But no, there will be no thrashings today, I haven't the time. I have two centuries of work to catch up on and I need your help, if you please, to get up and to it.'

Asa thought for a bit.

'OK,' he said.

'O-K?' said Tooth. 'What does that stand for?'

'Not really sure, but it means yes, I'll help you.'

'Good! Run up and find my razor, lad.'

'OK.' Asa turned and carefully made his way back to the stairs.

20

A Close Shave

When he got to the top of the stairs and stepped back out into the hallway, Asa stopped.

Did all of that really just happen? he asked himself. Was I really just talking to a two-hundred-and-fifty-year-old man who asked me to fetch him a razor?

The events of the last few days had been so unbelievable that he was now just about ready to believe anything. Then he remembered the sprite, whom he hadn't seen since the sneeze.

'Hello?' he called. 'Are you here?'

He found the creature back in the room with

all the junk and jars. It was hovering up near the ceiling and was clearly in a state of anxiety.

'It's all right,' he tried to reassure it even though he wasn't quite convinced himself. 'It's the old man, Benjamin Tooth, but he can't harm you, he can't move.' Asa explained what he had seen and was sure, even though the tiny sprite did not reply, that it had understood.

Asa started looking around for a razor but in amongst all the rusted tools and artefacts littering the shelves and worktops the only likely thing he found was a large pair of iron shears. The candle stub was nearly gone now so he found another and lit it.

'I'm going back down,' said Asa. The sprite hung in the air. 'Are you coming?' The creature didn't move.

'It was you that made me come here – I didn't want to, but now I've seen Tooth I can't just leave him here.' Still nothing from the sprite.

'Well, come if you want to,' he said and started

towards the door. Immediately the sprite was back at his shoulder as he cautiously descended the stairs.

The heap of silvery hair was still and silent again so this time Asa gave a polite cough. Again the sprite flitted away but this time only to a safe vantage point up on one of the high bookcases.

'Who's there?' demanded the hair-pile. 'Is that the baker's boy?'

'No, it's me again, Asa Brown.'

A pause.

'Who is the present monarch?' it demanded.

'Queen Elizabeth the Second,' replied Asa.

'Still?' said the old man. 'How long have I been asleep?'

'Five or six minutes,' said Asa.

'Oh. Make haste then, lad – did you find my razor?'

'I found these.' Asa held up the scissors.

The thin bony arm emerged again and parted the curtains.

'Those are sheep shearers,' said Tooth after a moment.

Asa explained that they were all he could find.

'They'll do for now, boy,' he said though he was clearly quite insulted. 'Mind you don't chop off my nose.'

'Me?' said Asa, realising for the first time that he was going to have to shear this grumpy fossil himself.

'Who else?' demanded the fossil. 'I can't see a thing.'

Asa stepped forward, wondering what he was going to find beneath more than two centuries of old man's hair.

'Not too much off the top,' snapped Tooth. 'And leave the curls. Do I still have curls?'

'Um . . . I think they're over there.' Asa pointed back towards the door where, at the farthest extremities of the silvery locks there remained a touch of auburn colouring and some tight curls.

'I don't think I can save them,' he admitted.

'Get on with it, boy!'

Asa carefully removed the tricorn hat and took up a handful of Tooth's hair, cut it with the shears and let it fall to the floor. Then another and another. He grasped one side of the ancient fellow's moustache and chopped through it, then the other side. He pulled out a bunch of the hair that fell thickly over his face.

'Ow! That's my eyebrow!' said Tooth but it was too late. He did the same to the other side and soon the ancient face started to reveal itself. It resembled a dried prune, tiny and wrinkled beneath the huge mop of hair.

Handful by handful the locks dropped to the floor until Benjamin Tooth sat there in a rickety wicker chair, blinking in the candlelight. His skin was leathery and creased, his body frail and thin, disappearing into an old frock coat that had probably fitted him many decades ago.

'How do I look?' he asked.

'Um . . . great,' Asa lied.

'Hand me a glass, boy,' he said gesturing towards a small table by his side that had been unearthed during the haircut. On the table were a notepad, a long clay pipe and a hand mirror, which Asa picked up and gave to Tooth.

He took it in his bony fingers and gazed at his reflection for a long time. Slowly his fragile body began to shake again but Asa could not work out from his expression whether he was laughing or crying. The shaking began to get more violent and he started to rock backwards and forwards in the chair.

'Heh heh heh!' a wheezy chuckle bubbled up from deep inside his dusty lungs but there was no smile on the wrinkly face. It sounded like an angry, bitter laugh and Asa stepped back. Tooth looked up at him with mad eyes.

'I got it wrong,' he hissed and his mouth stretched into a strange manic grin revealing a row of brown, stubby teeth. Two fell out and dropped into his lap.

'Got what wrong?' asked Asa.

'It didn't work! I thought it held the key to eternal youth but look at me! LOOK AT ME! I'M ... OLD!'

'But you're still alive,' said Asa.

'What's the point of eternal life if you still grow old?' spat the old man. 'They tricked me! The little devils tricked me! It's nothing but a torture device! It's an instrument of torment!'

'What is?'

The old man started to lift his other hand from where it had been resting in his lap covered in chopped hair. As he slowly raised it up and the hair fell away Asa could see that he was gripping the carved wooden totem from the pictures in the journal. His gnarled fingernails had grown around and into it so that he couldn't have put it down if he'd wanted to.

'This!' He shook the thing at Asa. 'THIS was supposed to keep me young forever. Instead it's turned me into a living corpse!'

Tooth was getting very angry now and as he spoke he spat his remaining rotten teeth across the room.

At this point the sprite broke his cover and dived down in a flash towards Tooth. It grabbed the top of the statue and pulled with all its might, not realising that the old man's fingernails were fused into it.

'AAAGH!' screamed Tooth in a spitting rage. 'Little demon! Get away from me or I'll pickle you in vinegar!' He swiped the statue this way and that as the sprite held on tightly, then he smashed it down on the table beside him. The sprite darted out of the way and circled round to land on the back of Tooth's hand where he administered a deep and painful sting.

'YEEEOOOW!' Tooth screamed and would have dropped the statue if he could. 'Spiteful swine! I'll kill the lot of you!'

Quaking with rage, he summoned all his strength and began to haul himself up out of the chair,

which up to now had been hidden. The clumps of hair fell away from what once may have been an impressively embroidered coat and breeches but now they were so rotten they resembled filthy lace and a cloud of moths flew up into the air in surprise. Tooth batted them away from his face and looked for the sprite.

'Where is it? Help me find the devil! I'll skin it alive! Where is it, boy?'

'I'm not going to help you kill it,' said Asa. Though he knew this would enrage Tooth even further he also knew that he could leave at any time and the frail old skeleton would not have the strength to follow.

'He's my friend,' Asa continued. 'He brought me here.'

'Your friend?' Benjamin Tooth was incredulous.

'Yes,' said Asa. 'He wants the statue back and I came to help.'

At this, instead of flying into another torrent of fury, the wind seemed to go out of Tooth's sails and he slowly sank back into his chair where he sat breathing heavily.

'It's mine,' he eventually said. 'I found it.'

'You stole it,' said Asa feeling braver by the second. 'I read your journals, I read how you destroyed their home and looted their treasures.'

Asa felt the sprite land on his shoulder, listening.

'Nonsense,' said Tooth. 'I was doing it in the name of science, in the name of human progress.'

'You were doing it to get rich and famous,' said Asa.

'But instead somebody else must have got rich and famous while I slept for two hundred years in this confounded chair. And now you're all "friends" and you live together in perfect harmony.'

Asa thought. 'No,' he said. 'Nobody else knows about them, only you and me.'

This was obviously a surprise to the old man and the ugly scowl left his face.

'Really? Nobody knows?'

'Nobody.'

'They've not been discovered? Written about? They're not kept as pets or in zoos?'

'They still live on the moor, in secret, and no one knows they are there.'

'Then how did you come to be here, boy?'

'I found one in my pond, after a storm. Then I found your journal.'

Tooth's head dropped on to his chest and he seemed for a long time to be thinking. Eventually he looked up again and raised his hand.

'Help me up, boy,' he said.

Asa stepped forward with the sprite still on his shoulder and offered his hand to Tooth, whose skin felt like paper, cold and dry. The old man eased himself up.

'Help me upstairs,' he said and took his first, unsteady step for hundreds of years.

'Lean against me,' said Asa, and they started to make their way to the stairs. Tooth looked at the piles of books, the broken shelves and the thick cobwebs.

'When did the cleaner last come?' he asked.

'Probably about 1790,' said Asa.

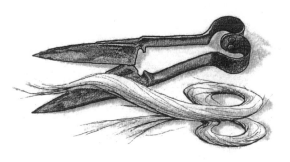

21

Redemption

It was slow progress up the stone steps to the house. Benjamin Tooth's thin frame could hardly support his ancient, moth-eaten clothes and Asa was worried that if he fell his bones would crumble under the weight.

Eventually though, they made it to the top of the stairs and Asa helped Tooth through the door into the hallway where he stopped to get his breath back. Tooth lifted his head and looked around at the derelict house, the rotten stairway and the piles of dead leaves.

'Oh my,' he whispered. 'I have been asleep a long time.'

A sadness softened his craggy features.

'I had so much I wanted to do.'

He leaned again on Asa and started towards the door leading to the room of artefacts and equipment.

'My laboratory,' he wheezed. 'Must get on . . . work to do.'

Once in the cluttered room Tooth hesitated again as he surveyed filth and mess. He sighed deeply.

'My work. How could it be?'

For the first time Asa felt a pang of sympathy for the old fellow.

'It's been a long time, Mr Tooth,' he said. 'Everyone thought you were dead.'

By now it was getting dark outside and the candle was the only source of light in the dingy room. Asa thought he saw the glint of a tear drop from Tooth's eye and roll down his ancient cheek. He gestured toward a large chair that still sat behind a great desk. Asa helped him hobble over and brushed the leaves and dust away. His bones creaked as he lowered himself into the chair and looked at the items on his desk. He reached forward and opened a large, leather-bound volume. But the paper was dry and brittle and flaked away in his fingers like confetti. He lifted an inkpot and turned it over but the ink had dried to a black stain and nothing dripped out. Tooth sighed miserably.

'Tell me about the future,' he said.

'The future?' said Asa.

'Yes, now, the present day. What happens in the time of Queen Elizabeth the Second?'

'Well,' Asa began, 'we have televisions now, and computers . . .'

'Tele-what?' Tooth interrupted.

'Television. It's a box with pictures on it, in it, moving pictures, we call them programmes.' Asa was aware that what he was saying must have sounded ridiculous.

Tooth was silent.

Asa continued. 'And we have cars and aeroplanes and helicopters . . . flying machines.'

'You have a flying machine?'

'Well, I don't have one, but there are, you know . . . you can go in them, buy a ticket and fly to the other side of the world in just a few hours.'

Benjamin Tooth slowly raised his hand.

'That's enough,' he said and sat in silent thought for a good long while.

Eventually he said, 'I'm tired. It's been an exhausting day.'

He thought for a while longer and then continued. 'My time here is long since gone. And I must give back what is not mine.' He lifted the hand that still gripped the sprites' totem pole so tightly. 'Help me take it back.'

'We can take it back for you, Mr Tooth.'

'No. I want to see my beloved Windvale Moor again. Breathe in the air.' Then he looked up with worried eyes. 'It is still there, isn't it? The moor? Have they built upon it? Is there a city in its place?'

'It's still there.' Asa reassured the old man and went over to help him up.

Once outside Tooth turned around to look at his house. The sight of the tree growing out through the roof seemed to amuse him and he tutted and shook his head.

They continued out of the gate and up a grassy bank, where Tooth stopped and looked for a long moment out across the moor. The sun had set but a bright band of blue still hung along the western horizon and a full moon was already high in the sky. The moor looked vast and wild and more beautiful in this light than Asa had ever seen it. He turned to Tooth.

'Where to?' he asked.

'Yonder.' The old man pointed to the crest of a hill some way off. 'But you'll have to carry me.'

Asa bent down and lifted the old man, cradling him like a baby. He weighed next to nothing and Asa felt as though he were only carrying a bundle of musty clothes. All this time the sprite was flitting

excitedly around, racing ahead and doubling back. Though he could no longer see them, Asa could sense the other sprites not far away, a hundred pairs of tiny eyes watching the progress of the odd-looking couple across the moor.

When at last they came to the top of the hill Asa set Tooth down on his feet and steadied him with his arm.

'Now,' said Tooth as he held up the twisted claw that held the fairy statue. 'Take it away.' Asa took hold of it and started to prise open the gnarled fingers and nails. He winced as the old man's knuckles cracked and some of the fingernails splintered and broke but Tooth didn't seem to notice – he was gazing at the landscape with a look of peace and calm.

At last Asa worked the statue from his grasp and the sprite flew down, reaching out a delicate hand to stroke the intricate carving. Then, looking down the slope, it gave a silent signal at which half a dozen others appeared and approached on cellophane wings. They took hold of the totem and lifted it away from Asa's hands, upward into the sky.

Tooth watched it go and nodded.

'It's as it should be,' he said. Just then, a wind stirred the grasses in the valley below and, with a soft rustle, it climbed the slope towards them. Benjamin Tooth removed his tricorn hat, closed his eyes and, as the wind passed by, his ancient body crumbled to dust and blew away on the breeze.

The ragged clothes fell to the grass and the last of the moths fluttered off to find a new home.

Suddenly Asa was alone and exhausted. He felt ecstatic and dreadfully sad all at the same time. He needed to rest before the long cycle ride home so he lay back in the long grass and stared up at the cloudless evening sky.

Asa awoke several hours later and took a few moments to remember where he was. The moon was directly above him and his clothes were wet with dew. He sat up, rubbed his eyes and looked about. All traces of daylight had gone but the orange glow of a distant town marked out the horizon and a billion stars peppered the vast dome of the sky.

But as Asa gazed he noticed a scattering of stars below the line of the horizon and as he watched he was convinced that they were moving. Way off in the distance the flecks of yellow light were gathering together and weaving over the grass in a line towards him. As they came closer more lights started to appear across the moor and moved in to join the procession. Closer and closer they came and soon Asa was aware of a strange music drifting on the breeze, a high, humming chorus of intricate harmonies like a thousand microscopic violins.

As the lights reached the valley below him and started to climb he was aware of more behind him and suddenly the music was all around. And then he started to make them out, sprites, thousands of them, and each one carried a tiny lantern with a single glow-worm inside. They fanned out in front of him, settling on the grass and gorse bushes or hanging in the air. Some were so high they mingled with the stars and some passed close enough to touch. Those that were close Asa could see were making the music by rubbing together the thorny ridges along their arms and legs and the glow-worms dimmed or brightened with each change of pitch. Asa watched in wonder as they gathered from all corners of the moor and surrounded him completely. Then the music changed to a low hum. Eight sprites came forward holding the rescued statue, which they set gently on the ground. The music rose again into a crescendo and the swarm parted to let through a single, magnificent-looking creature.

It was bigger than the others and its wings and limbs tapered to thin tendrils that snaked in the air. It looked older than the rest, with large, horny ridges on its skin and huge, iridescent eyes.

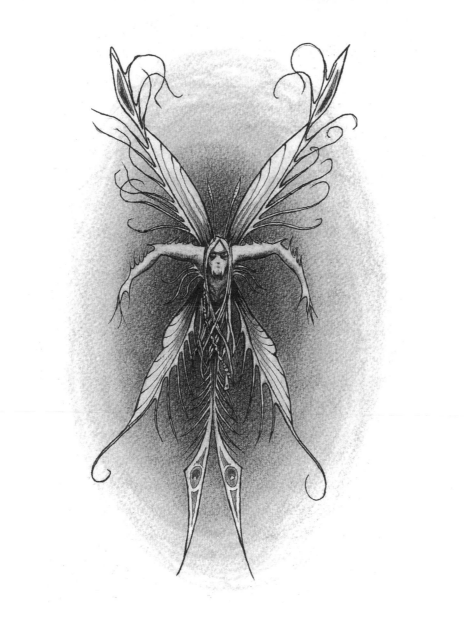

It hovered a few feet in front of Asa and seemed to be studying him carefully. Then it made a few gestures with its arms and several others came forward, carrying items which they laid at Asa's feet. He leaned forward and looked at the gifts, chords of woven thread and grasses, strings of beads and plaited strips of fabric.

The large sprite gestured again and one of the sprites came forward. Asa recognised his friend who pointed down to the trinkets on the grass. Then it flew in close, right up to his face so that its eyes were level with his, reached out and placed its hands on his temples. Asa heard a haunting, musical voice deep inside his head.

Thank you, it said.

Then, on an invisible signal, the whole swarm lifted into the air as one and came together in a huge luminous cloud above him. It morphed and shifted in the sky like starlings coming in to roost, before a thin line started to break away and snake back across the moor. Other lines snaked from this one and soon the points of light were dispersing in all directions across the landscape.

Asa watched until the last one had blinked out of sight, slowly gathered the gifts they had left, and got to his feet. He took one last look at the moonlit moor and turned to start the long journey home.